"And just ~~what are you doing?"~~

His strong f
hair and forc
covers. Vick
show you again." She started to edge back down but
was halted by the tightening grip in her hair.

"Do you think it's fair to attack a man while he's
down?" he pursued.

"You seemed to be rising to the occasion," she teased.

He cupped the back of her head in his palm and brought
her lips to his, kissing her with drowsy determination.
"That's a delightful way to wake up, sweetheart."

"It's a glorious morning that positively demands appreciation. I think you should get up and look outside," she urged.

He kissed her again, his lips warm and clinging. "The
part of me you were getting up does *not* look out
windows. Besides, are you sure we have time for what
your wanton actions would lead to?"

"Joe, we have all the time in the world..."

Mary Haskell *is a Yankee transplant from California.
Singer, actress, playwright, theatrical composer, world
traveler, and mother of three, she lives in a suburb of
Boston with her husband and their two Himalayan cats.
Outside of her family, her greatest loves are gardening,
gourmet cooking, music, and, most of all, writing.*

Dear Reader:

Spring is on its way—and so are more TO HAVE AND TO HOLD romances! We began publishing the line just six months ago, and already we've developed a dedicated and growing following, women (and even some men!) who love TO HAVE AND TO HOLD and buy all three books each month.

TO HAVE AND TO HOLD is the one romance line that's truly different. No other line presents the joys and challenges of married love. And TO HAVE AND TO HOLD offers the variety you crave—from love stories that tug at your heartstrings to those that tickle your funny bone. At the same time, you can trust all TO HAVE AND TO HOLD books to provide you with thoroughly satisfying romantic entertainment.

Your letters continue to pour in—and they're inspiring as well as helpful. All of you share our enthusiasm for the concept behind TO HAVE AND TO HOLD. Many of you also praise individual books and authors. From your letters, it's clear we've convinced you that, in TO HAVE AND TO HOLD, stories of marriage are as exciting and romantic as those of courtship. We're pleased and delighted with your response!

Warm wishes for a beautiful spring,

Ellen Edwards

Ellen Edwards
TO HAVE AND TO HOLD
The Berkley Publishing Group
200 Madison Avenue
New York, N.Y. 10016

To Have and to Hold

ALL THAT GLITTERS
MARY HASKELL

SECOND CHANCE AT LOVE
BOOK

Other books by *Mary Haskell*

Second Chance at Love
SONG FOR A LIFETIME   #124
REACH FOR TOMORROW   #144
CRAZY IN LOVE   #176

To Have and to Hold
HOLD FAST 'TIL DAWN   #8

To Have and to Hold books are published by
The Berkley Publishing Group
200 Madison Avenue, New York, NY 10016

To my country—
I wouldn't leave it either.

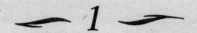

VICKI ROLLED ONTO her back and started her waking-up ritual. Right leg: point the toes and push. Left leg: point the toes and push. Mmm, nice. She shimmied down in the bed so she could straighten her arms above her head, brace her hands against the wall, and give her sleepy body the full-length stretch. Oh, did that feel good!

Now to hazard the next step. She raised one eyelid just enough to allow a glimmer of dawn's early light to slip under, then snapped it shut, deciding that dawn was highly overrated. Someday she wanted to be in a test group studying the effects of compulsory sleeping-till-noon.

Turning onto her side, she opened her eyes. Joe was sound asleep, lying on his back clutching the covers up under his chin. Funny, he looked like a smug professor about to deliver a lecture to an assembled dream class. By this time he probably *would* rather be delivering the lecture than sitting in the class taking notes.

Abruptly Vicki's mind clicked to fully awake. Joe! He was right here beside her in their bed. He wasn't out at the kitchen table surrounded by textbooks, having set the alarm for 4:00 A.M., or not having gone to bed at all, which had happened too often lately. A happy smile spread across her face. It was over. Her gaze flicked to the dresser, where his new master's degree was propped. He finally had it. Hip, hip, hooray!

She hoisted herself to one elbow, propping her chin on her hand. Taking her time, which was quite a luxury for her, too, she studied her husband's peaceful face. No wonder he looked smug. All those years of dedication to getting his M.B.A. had finally come to a successful end. She was so proud of him!

She smiled again, remembering Joe's blunt admonition on their first date: "I have to be honest. I can't get involved with anyone. I graduated from Harvard three years ago, and I've got a good job that's teaching me a lot about the world of commerce. But where I want to go in business will require a master's degree, and every cent beyond subsistence goes toward that goal. That's not exactly conducive to a lifestyle I'd want to ask someone to share. So we have to keep it light."

She flushed with pleasure at the memory of how those glistening blue eyes, those eyes that so visibly broadcast the intelligence behind them, had hungrily skimmed her face before Joe had added, "That's going to be a very hard thing for me to do."

It had been impossible for both of them.

She eased herself back to the pillow, not taking her eyes from that fine-boned, aquiline profile, that oh-so-beloved face. Joe. Josef Anton Beck. He had the features of an Austrian aristocrat, and why not? He was descended from a whole line of them. She slid over next to him, loving the feel of skin on skin, awestruck for the thousandth time at the luxury of having him so readily available to her. No matter how pressed for time, Joe made it clear that she had the permanent number one slot on his list of priorities.

You're a lucky lady, she told herself. Herself agreed.

She draped her leg over his, snuggling in the crook of

his arm to rest her cheek on his bare, lightly haired chest. Free. They were both free. His schooling was finished, and she had six whole weeks off, thanks to the end of the academic year and the willingness of the youngsters she counseled to discontinue their therapy for the summer. The morning took on a glossier sheen. The first shiny day of a bright new future. How could Joe sleep on a morning like this? He should be sharing the golden glow of this glorious dawn!

She kissed the underside of his firm, dominant chin, and he made a noise that was a cross between a grunt and a purr. Scooting her body fully on top of his, she lightly tongued the sensual mouth that belied the firmness of the chin. No response. Was he playing dead? With her thumb and forefinger she gently pried open one eyelid. "Are you in there?" she whispered. No answer. He *was* playing dead.

She'd fix him. Sliding all the way down under the covers, she kissed him in a way that was guaranteed to attract his attention. Instant reward. There was one part of him that couldn't play dead. Strong fingers twined themselves in her tousled hair and forced her up to meet his sleepily reprimanding gaze.

"And just what are you doing?"

She grinned at him impishly. "You mean you didn't get it the first time? Here, I'll show you again." She started to edge back under the covers but was halted by the tightening grip in her hair.

"Do you think it's fair to attack a man while he's down?"

"You seemed to be rising to the occasion."

He cupped the back of her head in his palm and brought her lips to his, kissing her with drowsy determination. "That's a delightful way to wake up, sweetheart."

"It's a glorious sunny morning that positively demands appreciation. I think you should get up and look outside."

"The part of me you were getting up does *not* look out windows. Besides, *you* are what fills my life with sunshine. That yellow ball in the sky is but a poor second." He kissed her again, his lips warm and clinging. "As for your method of getting my attention, I'm not complaining, you understand. But are you sure we have time for what your wanton actions would lead to?"

Vicki raised herself on both elbows, offering him a silly grin. "Joe, don't you remember? We have all the time in the world!"

The light of recollection crept into his eyes, then spread out over his face. "Vicki!" he yelped joyously. "It's true, isn't it? We finally did it!"

"*You* finally did it." She nestled her head under his chin as his arms encircled her.

"Oh, no, no way. This is a joint triumph."

"Joe, you'd have done it even if you'd never met me."

His arms tightened around her. "Honey, don't even say that. If I'd never met you—what an awful thought! What would my life be like without you?"

"Probably about the same: a dull old life full of constant successful work, constant overachievement, and constant comments by all those professors and fellow students about how brilliant you are. With one difference, of course. You'd have the added pressure of being constantly pursued by dozens of panting girls."

"Hmm. How about dozens of pant*less* girls?"

"That, too."

"I don't want dozens, just one . . . just the one I've got." He ran his hand over her smooth, warm back. She felt so good. He could never get enough of her. "You said one word back there that would sum up life without you: *dull*." He was startled by the wave of loneliness that washed over him at the mere thought of being without Vicki. And to think he had once come so close to convincing himself he should stop seeing her. What if his father hadn't jolted him back to good sense!

"Did I ever tell you what my father said about you the first time he met you? Remember? The time he and Mom came to Boston to spend Thanksgiving with me and took both of us out to dinner?"

She raised herself up on her elbows again, her interest

piqued. "I don't think so. What did he say?"

Joe affected a German accent and a stern tone. "He said, 'Josef, my son, marry this girl. Ask her tonight, and do not hesitate. She is just what you need.'"

Her eyes widened. "Your *father* said that?"

Joe loved watching Vicki's face. It was a mobile data screen of her thoughts and emotions. Her large, unbelievably green eyes always looked slightly awed, as though everything they saw utterly intrigued them. Actually, that was probably true. Vicki often did seem to see a great deal more in life, particularly in people, than he did. Vicki wasn't exactly beautiful, but she was the prettiest thing he had ever seen.

"Yes, my father said that. Behind that sober Germanic exterior is a discerning, clever mind."

"I know. Cleverness runs in the family. How come you never told me about that before?"

"No reason. I must have forgotten to. Besides, you know how much both my father and mother love you."

"Yes, I do. But somehow I can't picture him giving you that advice the first time he met me. He always seems so careful about making decisions. That also runs in the family."

"He takes after his son; he knows a good thing when he sees it. He told me I was too dominated by my oversized mind—and yes, he did say it that way—and that you would keep me human. He was, as he has usually been throughout my life, right."

"I love your father. I think he may be even smarter than his son. But you didn't take his advice. You waited until the following January to propose to me."

"That's because I thought it was unfair to ask you to marry a guy who lived like a pauper so he could use every spare dime to pay for graduate school. As you may have noticed, my need for you overcame all my scruples."

"Your need for me, as I recall, was already being satisfied by that time."

Joe was silent for a moment. He touched her soft hair, which curled in springy dark brown tendrils around her heart-shaped face. He felt overcome by his love of this woman who, just as his father had predicted, filled his days and his nights with joy and warmth and humor; who had a touching way of noticing, and bringing to his attention, the charming, quaint, or vulnerable traits in the people around them; of planning nice surprises for friends and relatives who seemed to be blue or lonely or, in Vicki's opinion, in need of a lift.

Vicki ran one finger across his slightly stubbly cheek. "You're awfully quiet. Are you trying to remember why you asked me to marry you when I was already inhabiting your bed?"

He kissed the top of her head, lingering long enough to savor the sweet smell of her hair. "I was thinking that I couldn't possibly count the number of my needs you satisfy. You know, it's strange, honey, how cut off you can get without even realizing it. That's what my father saw, and what my mother was always at me about. I would become so focused on a project or an idea that I'd almost forget there were people around. Not because I didn't care, but because I *forgot* to care. That's what my wise papa saw in you: a beautiful little bundle of solidly compressed humanness, who also just happened to be smart enough to more than hold her own. I love you so much, my darling Vicki. You make me feel complete. Does that make any sense?"

Vicki had to swallow hard before she could answer. "It more than makes sense. It echoes the way I feel with you . . . the completeness." This morning had indeed turned out to be shiny and new. It had been so long since they'd had the luxury of simply lying in bed, holding each other, sharing their innermost thoughts. She did so hope it would set a pattern for the years ahead.

When Joe spoke again, his voice held a note of longing. "I want to give you everything you could ever want, to lay the world at your feet so you can pick and choose the best from it and send the leftovers back for the rest of humanity."

"The rest of humanity might not appreciate that."

"Yes they would. They'd all agree you deserve it. I've

wanted to give you the best, and all I've given you is one hell of a grind, a chance to experience near-poverty, and lessons in how to live with stress. Honey, have you ever regretted marrying me?" Before she could answer he squeezed her and blurted, "Say no."

"No." She giggled. "So much for multiple choice."

He laughed, too. "Okay, multiple choice. Same question: yes, no, or Fifth Amendment?"

"Still *no.*" She snuggled even closer, full of the deep contentment she always experienced when his arms were around her. "Joe, hold me. Just hold me tight. You left that off your list, you know . . . how good it feels to be held by you—safe and secure and cared for. I grew up with so much love; it would've been disastrous for me if I'd married someone who never said 'I love you.' And it hasn't been such a grind. It's been fun, too. You may not believe that, but it's true. It's more fun for me to work along with you than it ever was to play with anyone else. I am completely satisfied with my position as Mrs. Josef Beck."

"Oh, you poor, besotted female. Your mind is addled from too much work and not enough relaxation." Cuddling her, he rubbed his cheek against her temple, his tone becoming serious. "Vicki, thank you."

"For what?"

"Most of all for loving me. Also for taking my dream on as your own. For understanding my refusal to take money from my parents or to let my Uncle Anton pay my tuition. The Beck pride. I needed to do it myself."

"I like your pride. Along with that pride goes honor and strength and a sense of responsibility." She couldn't help hugging him tighter. "And of course you couldn't take money from your dad. Since he retired, your folks have had just about what they need to live on. And I know why you refused your uncle's offer, Joe. You can't fool me. You thought it might hurt your father if you refused his money and took your uncle's."

"True. Dad could never convince himself that he shouldn't be able to overcome his rheumatic heart with sheer willpower. Having to retire early was a blow to his pride; he didn't need another from me."

"In all fairness, though, it must be frustrating for your uncle. He's worked so hard and built that—what do you call a business that big? A minor Austrian empire? Now he has all that money, and he can't even send help to his brother or his nephew because they won't accept it."

"Oh, I suspect Uncle Anton understands the Beck pride. He's reputed to have a full share of it."

"Well, maybe one of these days you'll be able to accept a gift from him. From what I've heard about Anton, that would probably please him."

Joe smiled above his wife's head. "Yes. It's possible that one of these days I'll be able to do just that."

The bedside phone rang shrilly, making both of them jump.

"That thing is so loud," Joe mumbled, picking it up.

An equally loud, raucous musical duet came over the line.

"Happy graduation to you, and Mrs. Beck, too,
We're sorry we missed it, but what could we do?"

"Who is it?" Vicki had rolled off her husband and was watching him quizzically.

"It's your sister," Joe replied, holding the phone away from his ear. Draping one arm possessively around Vicki's waist, he turned back to the mouthpiece and said distinctly, "The crazy one with the big stomach and the weird husband who sings off-key!"

Dual laughter pealed through the phone, which Joe held so Vicki could hear, too. "Congratulations, Joe! We hated to miss the big day, but travel was a problem."

"Excuses, excuses," Joe retorted, grinning. He liked Vicki's sister Evelyn and her husband Jeffrey. He liked her whole family: her mom and dad and three sisters and one brother and two brothers-in-law. It was one of the numerous benefits that had come with his darling Vicki—the large immediate family he'd never had. "Tell me, Evie, have you taken any weight off yet?"

"Yes!" The answer was yelled with such exuberance that Joe yanked the receiver farther from their ears.

"Really?" Vicki yelled back.

Jeffrey took over at the other end. "My wife," he announced in a regal tone, "gave birth to a seven-pound, three-ounce baby boy last night at eleven twenty-nine."

Vicki and Joe both yelped together at the news, babbling with enthusiasm over the first member of the family's next generation. When they finally calmed down, Joe asked, "What's his name?"

"Andrew, after Evie's father; David, after my father; Stoddard, after me."

"Look, Jeffrey," they heard Evie say, "the nurse is bringing him in. Joe," she called, "stay right there for a minute!" After a brief pause he heard, "Now, Andrew David, pay attention." Joe and Vicki exchanged puzzled looks. "Joe, I'm going to put the receiver next to the baby's ear. Say something to him."

"Evie," Joe said, "I should know better than to question your motives—I usually end up more confused than before—nevertheless, *why* do you want me to say something to the baby?"

"I'm hoping that the combination of his being born on your graduation day and having you talk to him on the first full day of his life might infuse some of your brainpower into him."

"Oh, deliver me!" Joe moaned.

"Now come on, Joe," Evie pleaded. "I know when *I* talk to you my mind always feels stimulated."

"Maybe that's not your mind, Evie. Maybe you secretly have the hots for me." He grinned mischievously at Vicki.

"Joe, be serious. How do you know I'm wrong? If Andrew grows up to be a genius, I'll have the last laugh."

"If Andrew grows up to be a genius, it will be a natural genetic development. You told me yourself that the only reason Vicki married me was that I was the first man she met who was smarter than she was."

Vicki gave him a playful punch.

"Good point. You can both talk to him. Double brain waves."

"Gitchy-gitchy-goo, Andrew," Joe said into the phone. "And grow up to be a genius to please your mother. Besides, you might land yourself a great wife like I did." He passed the phone to said grinning wife.

"Gitchy-goo for me, too, Andy-boy. And try to have bright blue eyes and yellow hair like your Uncle Joe's." She reached up to fondle the hair in question. "It'll do a lot for your chances of getting a great wife!"

Jeffrey was talking again. "Sorry about that, Joe, but you know all the women in this family are strange but wonderful creatures who must be catered to."

"Agreed." He gazed lovingly at Vicki.

"How did the graduation go? Did the rest of the family get there all right?"

"They sure did. It meant a lot to me that they'd come all the way from Ohio. It also means a lot to have you two call. And the graduation was great. Vicki and I are still reeling under the knowledge that it's finally happened."

"I don't doubt it. Well, congratulations again. We'll be in touch."

"Listen, the same to you. We'll be looking forward to seeing our new nephew!" Joe handed the phone to Vicki as Jeffrey relinquished his end to Evelyn.

"How are you, Evie?" Vicki asked. "Do you feel as healthy as you sound?"

"Of course. You'll see when you have kids; all that fresh Ohio air we grew up in holds you in good stead. I called Mom and Dad last night, and I'm about to call the others. Is everyone staying at the Marriott? I forgot to ask."

"Yes, you'll find them all there. We're meeting them for dinner tonight. Joe's parents are up from Florida, and I guess the whole gang is having lunch together and going in to do some touring of Boston. They insisted that we take the day to ourselves, for which I must admit I am most grateful."

Joe nuzzled her hair in tacit agreement.

"I don't blame you. You must both be pooped. Well, time to feed my son. Love, and love from Jeff, too, he says."

"Same here. Thanks for calling."

Joe replaced the receiver and flopped back on the pillow, pulling Vicki with him. "That's terrific," he said. "They've got a son. Just think, honey, we'll be able to consider starting a family before long, as soon as I get well enough established in a job for you to take a leave of absence from yours. Will you still be able to do that without endangering your position?"

"I think so. And anyway, it might be a good time for me to take an indefinite leave to do some work toward my doctorate. However, I don't want to think about any of that yet. We need to have a least a year, maybe longer, all to ourselves, without children, and definitely without textbooks."

"Amen to that. But I promise that when you're ready to go back to school, I'll make every attempt to help you as much as you've helped me. Although I won't be able to do your typing for you unless I take a crash course in it."

"Please, no courses of any kind right now! I think we've both seen enough of the academic world for a while."

"We've also seen enough of scrimping and saving and never having any free time. I still don't know how you stood it. I had my compulsion to carry me through. All you got when you married me was half the burden."

"I have never, for one moment, thought of my marriage to you as a burden." She ran a hand over the muscular arm clutching her waist.

"That's because you're a saint. So, I now declare this Saint Victoria day!"

"Saint, my fanny. A saint I ain't. A goddess, perhaps; a symbol of perfection, maybe; a sex symbol, without doubt. But a saint? Never!"

Joe touched her cheek with the tips of his fingers. "I love you so damned much."

She put her hand over his. "I'm so glad, because I love

you, too. Love you and need you."

He kissed her lightly on the lips. "All right, now. Since this is your honorary day, and there's nothing we *have* to do until we meet the family this evening, what would you *like* to do?"

"I don't care, as long as it's carefree and gay and fun. No serious stuff allowed."

"How about sex? Would that be too serious?"

"Sex is always allowed. But maybe we could find a new place. Somewhere outrageous where we've never made love before."

"Well, that excludes the bed, so maybe we'd better start the day by getting up and taking our showers."

"Why don't we take a shower together?"

Joe leered happily. "Sounds like a likely start."

Vicki extracted herself from his arms, bounced out of bed, went into the bathroom and turned on the shower, then brushed her teeth while she waited for the water to heat. The stall shower was small and cramped, like everything else in the apartment—a so-called mother-in-law suite in a Cambridge house. She and Joe had often joked that the owner must have wanted to discourage long visits. But the rent was reasonable, the neighborhood was fairly safe, and it was an easy commute to Harvard for Joe and to the office where Vicki was head of the counseling department for three elementary schools. They'd been fortunate to find the little apartment.

The steam was finally rising from the cubicle, so Vicki adjusted the water temperature and stepped in. Joe soon joined her, a large sponge in one hand and a bottle of bath gel in the other. "Now," he announced, "I am prepared, as the first step in Saint Victoria Day, to attend to your ablutions."

"I don't know that my ablutions need attending to," Vicki gurgled as the water weakly bounced off the top of her head and dribbled over her face and shoulders. She wished it would cascade, but the water flow in this place was, at best, a steady drizzle. "However, I have some other significant needs that are positively screaming for attention," she said suggestively.

"Well, I always like to start at the top." Joe put down the sponge and the gel and picked up a shampoo bottle. After pouring a substantial dollop into the palm of one hand, he worked the shampoo into a foaming lather in his wife's thick, short-cropped brown curls.

Vicki tilted her head back, relishing the tingling massage of Joe's fingers on her scalp. Closing her eyes more tightly to keep the soap out, she said, "We haven't had much time to talk the last few days, and you mentioned that two more companies were eager to interview you. Anything interesting yet?"

Joe started to answer, then, remembering the "nothing serious" rule that his wife seemed to have forgotten already, amended his reply. "Well, I've been screening the job offers as they flood in, and so far none of them seems quite adequate. Can you believe that there is not one, *not one* position in the president-to-CEO range among them?"

"Hmm . . . too bad." Vicki rinsed the last of the suds out of her hair while Joe washed his own. "And what, may I ask, is a CEO? It sounds like one of those foreign ministers who're always getting shot during revolutions."

"No, no, no. The CEO is the chief executive officer. Those are the guys who are up in the six-figure-salary range." He saturated the sponge with the perfumed gel and began to wash Vicki's right arm.

"Also the guys who make the big decisions, right?"

"Right."

"So that's where you'd like to be—the sooner the better, right?"

"Ah, my wife is very perceptive."

The sweet scent of the gel mingled with the steam and floated to her nostrils, further stimulating her senses, which were already sensitized by the rough texture of the sponge moving over her body.

"I suppose that might be too much to expect, being right out of school," Joe continued. "But what the heck, wouldn't you think there'd be at least one ninety-five-thousand-dollar a year vice-presidency available? Don't those corporate moguls out there realize how ready we are to sample the better-to-best things in life?"

Vicki was, at the moment, sure she was already doing that. Joe had finished lathering both of them, and as they stood huddled under the paltry stream of water, his hands took over the sponge's duty, systematically traveling over her, supposedly aiding the rinsing process. She was lost in her sensuous response to those hands, remembering the shock of their first touch.

She had met Joe at a large Fourth of July pre-fireworks party at a friend's apartment in the Harbor Towers in Boston. She shuddered at the memory of how close she'd come to passing it up. She had just finished graduate school at Wellesley College and was still suffering from exhaustion. The prospect of mingling with the crowds that crushed around the open bandstand where the Boston Pops Orchestra played while the riotous display of fireworks erupted over Boston Harbor did not hold its usual allure. She simply wanted to stay home and go to bed early. But the party was the last gathering of a number of her school buddies who were all set to return to their respective homes. Vicki was the only one in her gang who was seriously considering a very good job offer in the Boston area. Her memory blurred on the events of that party beyond the moment when her friend Joan had come up behind her and said, "Hey, Vicki, here's someone who wants to meet you."

Vicki lifted her face to the water, holding her breath as it coursed over her closed eyelids. Every second of that scenario was burned forever on her mind. The casual turn, while still laughing at a joke told by someone in the tight circle in which she stood. Holding out her hand with an automatic "How do you do" in response to the "Vicki Larsen, meet Joe Beck." Then he took her hand.

There was a song that was popular at the time; it was one long exultation about being touched by someone. Vicki had thought it the silliest thing she'd ever heard—until Joe took her hand and said, "I'm glad I found someone to introduce us." From that moment on, the lyrics of that song seemed far too restrained.

"Zo now, vee are clean, yes?" When Joe got playful, he adopted a pseudo-German accent. When he really wanted to tease her, he swung into actual German, which he'd learned from his Austrian immigrant parents. It always managed to drive her nuts. Vicki had no ear for languages and, try as she did, she seldom picked up more than a word or two.

Joe was guiding her out of the shower stall, rubbing her dry with one of their semithreadbare towels. "Vee now must pay attention to ze lubrication of ze various body parts, iss true?" He poured some skin lotion into his left palm. With the fingers of the right hand, he gently smoothed the lotion over her soft, flawless skin. "You know, honey," he whispered, "no matter how many times I touch you, it always surprises me."

"What does?"

"Your skin. I thought no one had skin like this past the age of six months."

She gasped. Those long, sensitive fingers were now rubbing lotion over her left nipple. "Actually," she breathed, "I rent it by the month from the mad scientist department at M.I.T. They replace it when it gets wrinkled. It's my one extravagance."

"I see." He stopped, looking down at the tips of her full breasts. "That cream didn't go on quite smoothly enough. I'd better do it over. And what do they charge for that service?"

"Oh, Joe, that feels so good." Vicki's knees wobbled as Joe meticulously reapplied the lotion. "The terms weren't too clear . . . something about the firstborn . . . oh . . . Joe . . ." He was on his knees, his hands covering her inner thighs with the warming balm.

"Son?"

"Hmm? Oh . . . no . . . million." She bent over, sinking her lips into soft, damp hair as he did the same.

"Vicki?" His voice was muffled.

"What?" Hers was shaky.

He raised his face to hers. "Have we ever made love on the bathroom floor?"

"Not that I remember."

"Is it outrageous enough?"

"Oh, yes."

"It's a good thing, because I don't think I'd make it to another location."

She glanced down and giggled. "I see what you mean."

His hands clasped her wrists, and he pulled her down before him, covering her lips with his. Vicki tilted her hips forward, pushing him to his haunches as she sank to her knees.

"Ah . . . Vicki . . ."

"I," she purred, "am impaling myself on your lust, making a sacrifice of my body to your sexual need."

"Finally," he growled, "I have bested those eggheads at M.I.T."

He dipped to take her nipple in his mouth as they rocked together. Vicki brought her parted lips to his throbbing temple, clutching his broad, muscled back for support as delicious sensations prickled through her.

"Ouch!"

"What's the matter?" She raised her head in time to see a grimace of pain cross his face.

"I've got a cramp in my leg! No, wait, don't pull away. I think we can solve this without disconnecting." Joe braced her while she straightened her legs and eased back to lie on the floor, half on the small round chenille rug and half on the linoleum. He followed her, curving his body into hers, all the while saying, "ooh, ow," then a loud, "damn!" when he banged his head into the doorjamb.

The waves of passion began to ebb into ripples of mirth, and Vicki started to laugh. "I'm beginning to think," she sputtered, "that this place may be *too* outrageous."

"Nonsense. For two people of our superior determination? Nothing is too outrageous!" He twisted around to take her nipple in his mouth while his fingers reached for what he called her "magic button." In so doing, he cracked his elbow on the jutting corner of the shower stall. "Oh, hell!"

By this time Vicki was convulsed with laughter. "Honey, I'm sorry, but this isn't going too well, is it?"

He looked down at her with a defeated grin, his chin braced on his fists, his elbows on either side of her ears. "Dammit, what's the use of being a genius if I fail at making love to my wife—especially on her special day!"

She reached up to brush a lock of wet hair from his forehead. "To me you are always a success, my darling. But perhaps we should eliminate the bathroom floor as a possible erogenous zone."

"Are you ready to call a halt and move to another location, or shall we stay here all day if necessary?"

"What an awful thought! I'm sure I have chenille-embossed buttocks already." By this time the situation had activated Joe's sense of humor, and he began to chuckle. "Joe, now stop that! If you start laughing, we won't be *able* to get up!"

He looked down at her, suddenly more serious. "How can you look so beautiful lying on an old linoleum floor?"

"I probably look ridiculous."

"No. Lovely." He nibbled along the ridge of her shoulder as his fingers found the spot they'd been searching for. "And loved."

"Joe, Joe, Joe." She wrapped her arms tightly around his neck and opened her mouth to his probing tongue. Their lips moved together, and their bodies took up the rhythm, the familiar, ever-joyous renewal of the passion that lived like a breathing part of their intense, all-encompassing need for each other.

He thrust into her, deeper and deeper, his hunger for her mounting, the hard floor and sundry hazards forgotten in the delight he felt in this woman he loved so much. "Vicki!" he cried as their bodies bucked at the same moment. Her moaning gasp sent him her message of fulfillment.

They lay for a while on that unlikely bed of delight, spent and too happily satisfied to move. When they finally rose, they stepped back into the shower for a quick rinse-off, just holding each other silently this time, each feeling so very blessed by their love.

After drying off, Joe went into the bedroom to dress while Vicki brushed and partially dried her hair. As she stepped through the doorway, she turned, bent over, and patted the bathroom floor. "I take it all back," she said.

"Hey," Joe called, "do that again. The view is marvelous."

"Lecher! I am married to a brainy lecher."

"Now, now, careful what you say or I won't tell you about the surprise I have for you."

"What?"

Vicki was a pushover for surprises. She had told him, with round-eyed excitement, about countless surprises her parents had given her and her sisters and brother while she was growing up. They had planned them carefully, knowing how much pleasure their children would get from them. Now Joe delighted in perpetuating the tradition, making a surprise occasion out of every event possible.

"Oh, Joe, tell me, please!"

He watched with pleasure as she jiggled with anticipation. "If you keep bouncing around in the nude like that, we'll end up back in bed and miss our breakfast at the Ritz."

Her expression telegraphed one big question mark. "Our *what?* Are you crazy? We can't afford to eat at the Ritz!"

"Not so. I've squirreled away a sou or so." He sneaked a sidelong peek at her as she stepped into her bikini panties, enjoying both her reactions and the view of her lovely, slim form with its long legs, tiny waist, and firm, round breasts. "How about wearing that pretty green dress, the one that matches your eyes?"

"Joe, are you serious about this breakfast? Are you already so eager to spend the money from that CEO job you didn't get?"

"It's all part of the surprise, to be revealed over eggs Benedict at the Ritz Grill."

"Joe, come on, tell! You know I can't stand suspense!"

"Not one word will be dragged from me until the proper

moment. So get dressed already." He grinned to himself as he reached into the closet for his one good suit. Even knowing it would make his wife ecstatic, he had kept this secret, without dropping a hint, for thirty-five whole days, and it was all but popping out of his pores!

2

JOE STOPPED THEIR battered old Toyota right in front of the entrance to the Ritz-Carlton Hotel. He got out and walked around to join Vicki just as the doorman helped her out of the car. Vicki stared in wide-eyed astonishment as Joe handed the keys to the parking attendant and said, "We're going in for breakfast."

Without blinking an eye, the young man took the keys and replied, "Yes, sir."

Such aplomb, Vicki thought. The attendant was probably wondering how anyone had the nerve to ask him to park an old wreck like that! Then she turned her attention to the prospect before her.

She loved eating breakfast at the Ritz. It had been one of the special treats she'd enjoyed when her parents occasionally came from Ohio to visit her during her years as an undergraduate, then a graduate student at Wellesley College.

Although her parents were certainly not wealthy, her father made a comfortable living from the drugstore he owned and ran in their small hometown. Her mother had always worked in the pharmacy with him, keeping track of inventory and doing the accounting, at which she was a whiz. She was equally adept at stretching their personal dollars, and they had managed, without financial disaster, to give their children not only love, values, and occasional discipline, but also a first-rate education.

After witnessing and participating in Joe's struggle to pay for his graduate degree, Vicki even more fully appreciated her good fortune. Her gratitude to her folks—and her wonder at their achievement—would never dim. Five college-graduate children, and her brother a doctor!

She smiled at Joe as he held the revolving door in place for her. No wonder the parking attendant had reacted so naturally to him. Joe had an innate elegance that clothed him in splendor no matter how threadbare his suit. She wandered over to gaze longingly at a sapphire and diamond bracelet displayed in a small window to the left of the entrance. "You know," she observed as he joined her and took her hand, "it should be easy for us to adapt to upward mobility."

"Oh? And what brings on that conclusion?"

"You look right at home in the lobby of the Ritz, and I feel right at home by your side. So as long as I stick with you, I'll be able to grow rich gracefully."

"Vicki, my darling, there is something about your logic that comes perilously close to your sister Evelyn's."

As Joe slid his hand up her arm and took her elbow, guiding her toward the grill at the far corner of the lobby, Vicki glanced up the curving staircase, then at the protruding showcase window just beyond its base. She stared for a moment at the stunning outfit displayed there, then tucked her worn purse more tightly under her arm to conceal it and glared down at the scuff mark on the toe of her right shoe. One of the first things she intended to do after Joe got started in a new job was buy a whole new outfit, head to toe and outer to inner. She was tired of looking like a walking ad for the local thrift shop.

The maître d' greeted them with a smile, picking up two

leather-covered menus before preceding them. They were
early enough to get a table by the window facing Newbury
Street.

Once seated, Vicki looked around, catching the eye of
a perfectly coiffed older woman seated alone at the next
table. The woman nodded graciously at Vicki, then turned
to speak with the waiter who had appeared at her side. She
seemed right at home, undoubtedly one of the permanent
residents of the hotel. An aged couple entered, paused at
the woman's table, and had a brief exchange. The man made
a courtly bow and sat at a corner table, unfolding his morning paper, while the woman, doubtless his wife, stayed to
chat for a few more minutes.

"Joe," Vicki whispered.

"What?"

"Can you even *imagine* ever having enough money to
retire at the Ritz?"

He smiled at her in that loving way that made her feel
so cared about. "If you want to retire at the Ritz, I'll see
that we can do it."

Why didn't she laugh when he made a statement like
that? Because she believed him. She honestly believed that
Joe could do anything he set out to do, a belief that was
clearly shared by many others. What was it that professor
had said, the one who'd been written up in *Time* magazine
and whom she'd been so delighted to meet at one of the
school socials? Oh, yes, he had told her that Joe had, along
with his superior IQ, a winning combination of concentration, energy, and drive—everything he needed to succeed
in the tough, competitive world of business. "He'll keep
your life interesting, Mrs. Beck," the professor had said.

He certainly has so far, she mentally informed the absent
professor.

She watched Joe's gaze dart about the room, taking in
the scene, a smile on his lips. His eyes were fascinating,
so bright blue that the pupils seemed starkly black in comparison. She smiled, remembering a kidding comment made
by one of their friends. "Joe'd better never go to war," Allan

had observed. "The whites of his eyes are so white against that blue that he'd draw enemy fire before he got out of camp!"

The effect of those eyes was powerful. When Joe looked at her, the concentration of his blue gaze was almost hypnotic. And when she watched him study, or even peruse the menu, his eyes seemed like magnets, drawing the essence out of what he read and stamping the information forever on that megabrain behind them.

He was a rare combination, her husband: brilliant, good-looking, and highly lovable.

When their waiter arrived, they both ordered eggs Benedict. She had prepared the dish once, but her hollandaise sauce had been a disaster. What luxury to sit back while one waiter filled the water glasses and poured coffee into the china cups and another placed glasses of fresh orange juice in front of them.

As soon as they were alone again, Vicki leaned toward Joe. "Okay, time's up. Tell me your secret!" One side of his mouth curved up, creating a deep dimple. That dimple was the one incongruous thing about Joe. Such an aristocratic face shouldn't have a dimple. But incongruous or not, it was there, and she loved it.

"Now, Victoria, have you no patience? Should we not delay our discussion until after we have consumed our eggs?"

His eyes were dancing now. Whatever the secret was, he was very excited by it.

"Josef Beck"—she tried to make her hoarse whisper menacing—"if you don't tell me right this minute, I'm liable to explode all over the table from sheer curiosity!"

The dimple deepened, and he looked just a little as if he might explode himself. With maddeningly slow deliberateness, he reached into his breast pocket, extracted a long white envelope, and placed it flap side up on the table.

Vicki hesitated for a moment, surprised by a strange chill that passed through her as she reached for it. Shrugging off the ridiculous twinge of reluctance, she picked up the envelope and turned it over. It was neatly addressed in a bold script she immediately recognized. It was from Joe's uncle

Anton. It had been mailed from Salzburg, Austria. Vicki's heart took a jump. Dared she hope? All the secrecy about this, and they had just been discussing Anton! It could be a check—one that Joe had decided to accept.

With trembling fingers, Vicki lifted the envelope flap and pulled out the contents.

Joe watched the expression of incredulity that took possession of her face as she examined the enclosures. His own heart was pounding in his chest as he waited for the enormity of what was in that envelope to fully penetrate Vicki's mind. He wasn't surprised that it was taking so long. He had reacted the same way, going through all the stages from incredulous befuddlement to disbelief to uncertainty . . . and then to complete, unconditional acceptance.

The idea of waiting before sharing it with Vicki had come gradually. His first instinct with everything, good or bad news, was to race to her with it. But the last few months had been so grueling for both of them. He knew his wife so well; she had been on a heads-down, let's-get-it-over-with roll. With adamantly cheerful determination she had put in her own long, demanding days of counseling troubled children and coordinating department schedules, then come home to help him with research, with questions, with the aid of her nimble fingers turning out reams of typewritten pages.

He had forced himself to think about this missive for two days before making a decision. Mental discipline was his strong suit, but that had really been tough. Tougher still was the conclusion he had reached. He had decided that when Vicki was faced with the wonder of this gift, all the difficulties should be behind her. He wanted her to step off the treadmill directly onto cloud nine.

Neither of them really noticed the waiter put the plates with the eagerly anticipated eggs Benedict in front of them. Joe could feel his own excitement mounting, his own smile broadening as a mirror reflection of Vicki's face.

"Joe." Her voice was a mere whisper. "Joe, is this what I think it is?"

"Yes." For just one split second, he was afraid she might

faint. He reached over to cover her hand with his. "Are you all right?"

"I'm not sure. I think I'm in paradise. Does that mean I'm dead?"

"Maybe. But if so, I'm here with you, so we can enjoy it together."

"Joe, these are two round-trip tickets to Europe, made out in our names." Her gaze flew to his. "Aren't they?"

"Right."

"And one, two, three hotel confirmations in Switzerland?"

"Still right."

"And they all have three lovely words on them: *Paid in advance*."

"Nice, eh?"

"What does the letter say?" The letter was written in German.

"Well, aside from the congratulations, and greetings to you, the letter holds a couple of conditions for the gift." The panic on her face compelled him to continue quickly. "Nothing you'll mind too much, I'm sure. Anton is giving us the trip as a graduation present. He'd like us to spend the first few days with him in Austria and also come back to visit at the end of the trip. He says it would give him a chance to get to know us."

Her eyes were so round they looked like huge green marbles. "You mean we get to go to Austria, too?"

"Yep." With exaggerated casualness, Joe reached into his pocket and brought out another folded piece of paper, which he handed across to Vicki. "This was in the letter, too."

She opened it up, then shrieked, "Oh, my God!" She clapped her hand over her mouth and glanced sheepishly around. The other patrons quickly returned to their own business. "Joe!" The hoarse whisper was back. "Joe, this is a check for a thousand dollars!"

He nodded. "For expenses."

She stared at the check and the tickets and the reservations, then at him. He watched in fascination as her eyes narrowed and her hand clutched the papers so tightly they crinkled.

"Can we keep them?"

Joe laughed out loud at that. It hadn't occurred to him that she might wonder, though in light of the conversation they'd had earlier about the Beck pride and his reluctance to accept money, it should have. "Yes. I *had* planned to send them back with an irate note, but after your observation this morning that my rich uncle might *like* to give me a gift, I decided to be kind about it."

"You weren't—" She gave an exasperated sigh. "Oh, you're kidding me."

"Yes, I'm kidding you. I've already written to thank him, and I told him I wasn't going to tell you until the day after graduation, so you could start enjoying the idea right away." Joe leaned forward, the feigned nonchalance gone, his face aglow with enthusiasm. "Isn't it about the greatest gift you've ever heard of?"

Her green eyes were still wide with awe. "I've never known anyone who gave presents like this. In Ohio they give things like watches or stereos for big occasions." Pausing to pick up some of the nonchalance Joe had dropped, she added, "Such a thoughtful gift! How could your uncle have known that we'd always wanted a check for a thousand dollars? So much more appropriate than a pair of bookends!"

"Oh, I don't know. We do have a lot of books." He glanced down at her hands on the table. "Honey, if you don't loosen your grip on that check, it's going to need ironing."

She looked down, laughed, and reluctantly eased her grip. As she passed the envelope and check back to Joe, her mind chugged jerkily into the next gear. "Joe! How did he know?"

"That we wanted a thousand dollars?"

"No, that the place we both wanted to go to the most was Switzerland."

"Ah." His own nonchalant air was back. "Elementary,

my dear Vicki. My parents, of course. Don't you remember a year ago Christmas when we went to Florida to be with them? We spent one full evening talking about places we all wanted to travel to. Mom and Dad wanted to see Wyoming and Montana, and you and I discovered that we'd both always wanted to see Switzerland. Me because of the Alps, and you because of the strip show in Geneva one of your friends told you about."

"Joe Beck! That was not the reason." She grinned. "Well it wasn't the *only* reason." Her gaze dropped to her plate. "Oh, honey, look. Cold eggs Benedict."

Joe motioned to the waiter, who rapidly approached the table. With his devil-may-care aura in place, Joe said, "I'm afraid we let these get cold. Would you bring us another order, please?"

"Joe!" Vicki hissed.

The waiter didn't bat an eye. "If you'd prefer, sir, I could just have these heated quickly in the microwave. They would taste fine, I'm sure."

"Thank you, we'd appreciate that." When the waiter left, Joe smirked. "See? Nothing to it, kid. Stick with me and you'll be eating warm eggs and wearing carrots the size of diamonds."

Vicki sank back against her chair, suddenly drained after the highly charged experience. "I can't believe we're really going to Europe. Hey! *When* are we going?"

"Exactly five days from today."

"Oh, Joe, wait until we tell everyone tonight!"

He looked a bit embarrassed.

"Don't tell me they all know!"

"Well, my parents knew, and evidently your parents called them to confer about graduation presents—you know how they do at Christmas and all, so they don't overlap—and . . . well, I guess one thing led to another."

"You mean everyone knew but me?"

Joe's expression was a combination of concern and indulgence. "Honey, your parents have been springing surprises on you your whole life, and I've been aiding and abetting since I found out how much you enjoy them. This just happens to be a bigger surprise than most."

Vicki was still in a state of shock. "You can say that again."

The waiter reappeared with their steaming eggs and placed them on the table. Joe and Vicki grabbed their forks, their eyes catching in a smile as they both realized at once how hungry they were.

"Boy, does this look good." Vicki got a piece halfway to her mouth and paused to say, "I'm still dying to see the family tonight. It's going to be such fun to jump up and down and scream."

"Great. I've always wanted to be thrown out of the Marriott."

The rest of the day passed in a dazed this-can't-be-real marathon of planning, making lists, and trying to figure out how much of the thousand dollars they could spend on a few new clothes for the trip. The time to leave for the Marriott was upon them in unbelievably short order.

As they were riding up the escalator in the modern hotel, Joe looked around and commented, "This must be costing everyone a bundle. We should have taken the time to find them a less expensive hotel."

"Joe, you forget. They wanted to stay here, and I don't blame them. They don't travel that often, and I'm sure it's more fun, as long as they were going to be in Boston, to have a nice room on the waterfront."

Joe stopped at the top of the moving staircase, stepping to one side as Vicki joined him. "You're right. None of them travel much. My father's only been back to Austria twice since he left. Your folks have never been to Europe, have they?"

"No."

"Have any of your sisters or your brother been?"

"No."

"Makes me feel sort of funny about going in there and making a big thing out of this trip. Not so much with your sisters and brother, because that's different. But our parents . . ."

"Joe, honey, come on." She reached out to touch his cheek. "You know darn well that your father's health is the main deterrent to his traveling, and as for my folks, they've never seemed all that interested in Europe. Their life centers around their friends and local get-togethers. Midwesterners, well, they stay closer to home. They like it there."

He nodded. "I guess you're right. It's just that things are going so well, it makes me a little uneasy."

"Josef Beck, I can't believe you. For all your powers of deductive reasoning, you're so superstitious!"

"Listen, as you know, people who have lots of brains don't always have good sense. Don't gloat just because you have both." He took her hand. "Come on, pretty lady. They're probably wondering where we are. You know my father: If you say you'll be there at seven, you're late at three seconds after." They walked down the hall checking the numbers on the doors. "You did say they were all gathering in your folks' room?"

"Yes . . . oh, there it is." Vicki knocked, heard "come in," and opened the door. Pandemonium broke loose. She was grabbed from all sides at once by her sisters, Josie and Gerri, and her brother, Greg. She could barely see her mom and dad, great smiles on their faces, embracing Joe. Her brother-in-law, Lou, stood off to one side, grinning and waiting his turn. He was obviously used to this warm, slightly crazy family. She thought she spotted Joe's parents behind hers.

"Vicki! We just heard about it this morning! Oh, Lord, you must be ready to split your britches!" Her just-twenty-one-year-old sister Josie was jumping up and down in excitement.

"I am! Can you believe it, Josie? And you're the one who told me no good could come of marrying an egghead!"

"So I was wrong. I'm looking for one myself now. One with an Austrian uncle!"

Vicki went over to hug Joe's parents, who stood in the

midst of the Larsen maelstrom like two wooden soldiers trying desperately to learn how to bend. "Hello, Papa, Mama. You look lost in this madness. Are you wondering how your dignified son got caught up in such a group?"

Maria Beck hugged Vicki tightly. "We are so happy to see our Josef enclosed in so much love. Ah, Vicki, the sun shines in your face. Josef told you the good news, yes?"

"We are so glad for you." Rudolph took his turn to hug Vicki, who had quit trying to keep the tears from flowing down her face. "You and my son have worked so hard, so long. I am sorry—"

"Don't you dare finish that sentence, Rudolph Beck!" Vicki lightly placed her fingers on his mouth. They had made it clear that she had become the daughter they were never able to have, and she returned their love fully. "You helped Joe through four years of college, and that was a lot. Besides, he feels just as proud at having done this on his own as you would."

Rudolph smiled, his own eyes misting, and nodded. "Yes. And there is foolishness in looking backwards. Life holds just today and, with luck, tomorrow."

Before he could say anything else, her brother Greg yelled, "Attention, everyone! Dad wants to offer a toast."

They all found places to sit, on the beds or the chairs or the floor. Vicki could hardly see through her happy tears as her solid, good-looking, Rock-of-Gibraltar father stood.

"First of all, has anyone offered the guests of honor a drink?"

There were hoots of laughter and razzing of Greg, the appointed bartender. She and Joe were soon holding drinks, seated side by side on the edge of one of the double beds. Joe glanced at her and pulled a handkerchief out of his pocket to hand to her. He looked as if he'd need it back any second.

"I want to propose a toast to Josef, one of our acquired sons," Andrew Larsen said, raising his glass. There was a cheer from the other "children." "Joe, you've done remarkably well. You've set your goals and never wavered.

You've gone through one of the toughest graduate schools in the country and not only earned your master's degree, but done so at the top of your class. Our congratulations." Another cheer. "Even more admirable than that is the determination you've shown, the dedication that's held you on your course, and your extraordinary good sense in marrying our daughter!"

The room erupted in laughter, and Joe called out, "I'll drink to that" before leaning over to plant a light kiss on Vicki's lips.

"We're proud of you, Joe. Proud and happy to have you in our family. Vicki has always kept us on our toes, as you well know. I suspect she now keeps you on yours."

This won an appreciative smile of agreement from Joe.

"She has warmed our hearts and our lives with her unflappable optimism, and she's astounded us with her own academic achievements and her swift progress in her work. I have to admit that when she told us she wanted to marry you, we had moments of doubt. No parent *wants* to see a daughter take on what will clearly be years of hardship. But the doubts soon vanished. You've been a good husband to our daughter; we've never seen her happier. Maybe she thrives on hardship."

There was more laughter, accompanied by a bit of nose-blowing. Joe took the handkerchief back from Vicki.

"You brought us another dividend. You added to our family your wonderful parents. It has been our joy to share most holidays with them for the past three years, and we look forward to many more. They're still a little stiff and proper, but we're working on that."

Rudolph threw his head back and laughed, and Maria clapped her hands in delight.

"So, to come to the end of this long-winded toast. To Josef, on this great occasion. Our congratulations and our love!"

"Hear! Hear!" They all jumped to their feet and turned to Joe, recklessly clinking glasses and drinking the toast. Joe blew his nose.

Greg's voice rang out again. "Quiet! It's Rudolph's turn!"

It took a few minutes for everyone to settle down again. Then Rudolph stood. The room grew still. Rudolph had a presence, an Old World dignity, that Vicki often suspected he would sometimes like to shed.

He cleared his throat and looked down at the floor. When he spoke, his tone was soft. "My son. He has brought to me, and to my Maria, such joy. The pride I feel"—his hand went to his chest—"it strengthens this heart of mine."

Vicki looked over at Joe. Tears were running freely down his cheeks now. She reached over to take his hand, and his fingers closed tightly around hers.

"I am so proud, Josef, so very proud." Father and son looked at each other through tears of mutual love.

Vicki waited, expecting the usually reticent man to sit down, but to her surprise he continued.

"Also I would like"—he glanced over at the weeping Maria—"my wife and I would like to say the deep happiness we have from our times with all of you. When we came to this country, so many years ago now it does not seem possible, we felt so much alone. We were such children, eighteen, nineteen . . . we did not even have the English language. But my family wanted me out of Europe. My health was a problem; they feared to have me stay with the trouble coming."

Vicki studied the faces of her family. They were all fascinated. This was the first time any of them had ever heard this from Rudolph.

"So we made our lives here, with help from my uncle and aunt. Your country welcomed us, opened to us its arms. We are much blessed. Now you have brought back to us the big family in which we grew up."

The room was in danger of being flooded.

Then Rudolph turned directly to Vicki. "And Victoria. I do believe that our Josef, he looked and looked to find for us the perfect gift. The perfect daughter. You are a blessing, to us and also to our son, who found the perfect wife. He needs you. You will see, when you meet Anton, what I mean. Anton has a heart the size of his bank account."

They all laughed. They'd heard of Anton's bank account.

"But he has the same problem that you might have had, Josef. Anton, he wants to touch others, but it is for him a problem. To build the empire, to make the great fortune, is easy. But to share his heart, ah . . . not so easy. Anton, I fear, is a lonely man. You will brighten his days while you are there. Take care—he will want to keep you."

Joe and Vicki smiled at each other. This was a new view of the fabled Anton.

"Anton, he once had a wife who opened his heart. But she died so young . . . Maybe you can show him how to be with his daughter as your father and mother are with you." As though just realizing that he was still surrounded by people, Rudolph cleared his throat again, and his face reddened slightly. He raised his glass self-consciously. "Now, to our son and our daughter. Long life, continued love, and much success!"

They all crowded together, hugging, kissing, saying thankyou's. Joe went to his parents and took each of them, in turn, into his arms for a long, silent embrace. He then looked at each of those beloved faces and asked, "Are you sure it didn't upset you that I took such a large gift from Anton?"

His mother stood on tiptoe to kiss his cheek. "Josef, we are so glad for you, for you and Victoria. You are needing rest, and a little fun. And Anton must be so pleased to do it for you."

"Yes, your mother, she is right." Rudolph put his hand on his son's arm. "I know why you never let him give you the help for school. It was brave of you and kind and just a bit foolish. Your father is not as easy to hurt as you might believe. But now that it ends, the long struggle, I believe it's better you did it that way, by your own labors. A man needs to know of what he is capable." He patted Joe's arm. "Anton is a good man, Joe. I love my brother. He has, it is certain, enclosed in this gift his love. It is sometimes the only way he knows to send it."

Rudolph's eyes took on a faraway expression. "He only comes here to see us once, because he fears the flying. So

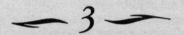

3

"HEY, WHAT ARE you grinning about?"

Vicki jumped. She had been so completely lulled by the jet's drone and so engrossed in her reveries that Joe's voice startled her. She reached over to take his hand. "That's a silly question. The same thing I've been grinning about for the last five days."

"You've seemed pretty happy, all right."

"*Happy* is an inadequate word. I need a word that means about twenty-five degrees above ecstatic."

"Like orgasmic?"

"Joe, shhh!" She glanced around nervously, then punched his arm. "Will you behave?"

"Why change my pattern now? After all, we're not doing too badly. Look where we are!"

Vicki looked out the window at the mounded clouds below. "I'm not entirely sure where we are. I mean, my mind knows we're in a jet, soon to land in Salzburg, Austria, but my psyche is still in shock."

"I don't wonder. So is mine. I hope I recognize Anton

from his pictures. I was only five when he made his one visit, and all I remember is that he seemed awfully tall."

"Who doesn't to a five-year-old?"

"Are you looking forward to meeting Anton and Gretchen?"

"Yes, I really am. I hope they speak enough English for me to communicate with them."

"I've talked to Anton on the phone, but of course the conversations are always in German. Dad says he speaks some English, though I really don't know how much. However, also according to Dad, he sent his daughter to the American school, which I understand is pretty much the norm these days. So at least you should be able to talk to Gretchen."

"I've seen a few pictures of Anton, but only a couple of old ones of Gretchen as a teenager. How old would she be now?"

Joe thought for a minute, then looked at her and frowned. "That's strange. I know so little about Gretchen. I understand she's very bright..."

"What a surprise."

He laughed. "That shouldn't bother you. You're very bright, too."

"There's bright, and then there's *bright*. But her intelligence won't bother me." She grinned at him. "I'm used to being around geniuses."

He took her hand and kissed the tips of her fingers. "Anton sent a notice about Gretchen when she graduated from the university, where she evidently captured all the top honors."

Vicki gave a dramatic moan. "Another one!"

Joe's eyes narrowed. "Hey, I hadn't thought of that. She might be smarter than I am!"

"Poor baby. Would that upset you?"

"Hell, yes! She's only a woman!"

"Josef Beck..."

He cringed, laughing. "Don't strike me. I'm innocent! I'm only kidding!"

"Okay, come on, what else do you remember? We'll be landing soon, and I want to know all I can before we meet them."

"Well, let's see. Gretchen's either the same age I am or a year older. I can't quite remember. So that's twenty-seven or twenty-eight. She's worked for her father for six years—part-time during school, then full-time. She got married a couple of years ago... The guy is older, about ten years, as I recall. He's a well-known surgeon. German, I think." He turned to her, looking very smug. "How about that? A regular font of information!"

"You are indeed."

The seat belt sign went on.

"Honey," Vicki said nervously, "do you think you could teach me to speak German in the next five minutes?" She hastily refreshed her lipstick and smoothed down her skirt. She felt a surge of pleasure at the sight of her handsome outfit—brand new, head to toe and outer to inner.

The plane bounced once, then settled to a smooth glide, and Vicki released her breath. They were here. She couldn't believe it. She looked out at the ring of mountains as the plane braked sharply, then crawled toward a low, nondescript building off to the left. Somehow she had expected the Salzburg airport to have turrets and bell towers and an orchestra seated on the edge of the runway playing Mozart symphonies.

When the door was opened and the line of people in front of them began moving, Vicki turned to Joe. "Joe," she whispered anxiously, "does my hair look all right?"

Joe squeezed her shoulder and gave her a reassuring smile. "You look beautiful." She did. But then, to him she always looked beautiful. She was the best thing that had ever happened to him. He moved closer behind her. Staying near your other half for added strength? he asked himself. Better believe it, he thought. Being close to her did make him feel stronger. He wasn't surprised that Vicki was nervous, but he was surprised at how jittery he was. Anton the empire builder had become something of a legend to Joe, and the legend was about to become real.

The luggage retrieval and the stop at passport control went quickly. As soon as they passed through, Joe spotted Anton, clad in a loden green lapel-less suit, with a huge smile on his face. Joe noted with humor that Anton had been studying a snapshot, which he quickly shoved into his pocket.

"Josef!" He waved a hand, the smile extending.

Joe grabbed the two large suitcases, Vicki grabbed the carrying bags, and they headed toward him.

Vicki stood back and let the two men have their moment together, grasping arms, patting shoulders, finally clasping each other in a hug. In the flesh, Anton was something of a shock. Joe's father was about five feet ten and had dark brown hair. Anton stood eye to eye with Joe's six two, and his blond hair and blue eyes were duplicates of Joe's. He looked far more like Joe's father than Joe's father did.

With a final slap to Joe's arm, Anton turned to her. "Ah, so I have the pleasure to meet Victoria. As pretty as the picture."

She gazed up at him in fascination. The magnetic blue eyes and the smile were so familiar. It was startling, like seeing a future vision of Joe.

"Welcome, welcome," he intoned. His accent was pronounced, his speech a bit hesitant.

"How do you do, Herr Beck. It's so wonderful to be here. How can I ever thank you?" The reply sounded stilted, but she'd heard that most Austrians were very formal, and she was walking a mental tightrope between adequately expressing her gratitude and observing unfamiliar protocol.

He waved his hand, as though brushing aside the need for formalities. "Please, please. Uncle Anton. We are all family, yes? And Josef has written so many the thank-you's. It was my pleasure to do."

His smile was infectious, and Vicki felt her wobbly knees sturdy up a mite.

"And now you meet my daughter."

Gretchen was a surprise. She looked entirely different

from the rather dowdy old snapshots Vicki had seen. She was striking. Tall, about five feet eight or nine, she had extremely short dark brown hair and was wearing an extremely chic suit.

Gretchen held out her hand. "Victoria, it is nice to meet you." The English was flawless, but the smile was strained. Maybe she was nervous, too. "I apologize that Conrad is not able to be here. He had the duties at the hospital." Conrad? Of course, Conrad Raab, her husband.

Gretchen then turned to her cousin Joe. She hesitated just a split-second before offering her hand. The smile became more strained, and the strain crept into her voice as she dutifully greeted him.

What's wrong? Vicki wondered, watching closely. She had one of her quick flashes of intuition. Gretchen didn't want them here. That's silly, she scolded herself. Why wouldn't she? But the hunch held, and Vicki's knees returned to wobbly.

Within minutes their luggage was in the trunk of the roomy BMW parked at the curb. They drove a short distance on the main road, then turned left and immediately began an ascent into the mountains. Vicki tore her gaze from the enticing scenery and concentrated on the woman sitting beside her in the rear seat. "This is so exciting to me," she offered. Then she inwardly groaned. The sensation of being a gushing schoolgirl visiting rich relatives was a bit too close for comfort. "I've never done much traveling, and I've heard that Salzburg is one of the prettiest cities in the world."

"Yes, I think that is true." Gretchen seemed reluctant to meet Vicki's eyes. "We will have a tour of Salzburg while you are here, of course, and we have arranged to attend one of the concerts there. It is too bad you will not be here for the festival. That is a truly inspiring spectacle."

"Gosh, just the scenery is inspiring." She *was* gushing. What was it about Gretchen that unnerved her? "Your English is perfect. I must apologize in advance. I'm afraid my German is nonexistent."

Gretchen's mouth moved, more a nervous twitch than a smile. "We all learn to speak English now. It is the international language in business."

"I understand you work with your father."

The hazel eyes darted to hers. "I work *for* my father."

Vicki saw a flash of anger in the glance that touched her, swung to the back of Joe's head, then dropped.

Momentarily startled to speechlessness, she fished desperately for another topic of conversation. "Do you and your husband live near your father?"

"We live quite near, in Bad Reichenhall. It is just across the border in Germany. We pass through it to get to Father's house."

Vicki tried desperately, but unsuccessfully, to call up a mental picture of a map of Europe with neatly outlined borders. All she could imagine was a black line across a road with a sign saying "Germany" on one side and a sign saying "Austria" on the other. Suddenly her lack of interest in history and geography was bobbing up to haunt her. She felt like such a foreigner in this country of her husband's heritage. And worse, a dumb foreigner. She'd have to get as much information as she could out of history-buff Joe.

The car stopped, and Vicki saw two towheaded Aryan-looking uniformed guards approach. They asked a few questions in German, and Anton held out his hand for their passports. The guard sternly studied the documents, and Vicki felt a cold chill run through her as scenes from TV reruns of old World War II films flashed through her mind. The guard handed back the passports, said something to Anton, and laughed, and Vicki's ominous image of him instantly dissolved. He was just a nice-looking kid doing what must be a rather boring job.

She was amazed at how soon they stopped again to go through the border-crossing routine. Somewhat timidly she asked, "Am I mistaken, or did we just go through Germany and back into Austria in the last ten minutes?"

The first hint of a smile touched Gretchen's lips. "Yes. It is confusing, I know, to one whose country goes on forever. We are now in Unken. It is not much farther."

As they wound through a neighborhood of handsome houses, Vicki listened to the two men in the front seat eagerly talking to each other in German. She realized she had never really heard Joe converse in German this way. The Becks politely stuck to English when she was with them, except for short exchanges. It was strangely unsettling to hear the fluency with which her husband spoke this language. It made him seem... well, just a bit alien.

Anton stopped the car in front of an iron gate, got out, unlocked the gate, and swung it open. The driveway ran up rather steeply, then leveled off in front of a spacious three-car garage. The two-story house, with a sharply pitched roof, sat on a plateau cut into the hilly terrain. Anton got out to open the doors for the women and take the bags out of the trunk.

The moment Vicki stepped out onto the asphalt surface her attention was captured by the fairy-tale splendor of the sweeping panorama before her. "It's incredible!" she gasped.

Anton's face lit up with pride as his gaze followed hers. "Yes. Our Austria, she is *herrlich.*"

In response to Vicki's inquiring glance, Joe said, "Magnificent."

She smiled, nodding in agreement. "It is indeed. *Herrlich,*" she repeated. "That sounds like an appropriate first German word for me to learn. I have a feeling I'll be using it a great deal."

Anton touched her arm, an almost shy gesture. "I am hoping you will love our land. It is of importance to me."

"I'm sure I will. How could I help it?" She waved her hand in an encompassing gesture toward the scenery. "It's awesome. Am I looking at Austrian mountains or German mountains or both?"

Anton laughed. "We will claim all. Why not? The borders they move, this way, that way, through the times."

Vicki took a moment to drink in the scene while luggage was carried in and the car parked. They were cradled in green and blue glory. Standing on the side of one mountain,

she looked across a wide, sparsely populated chasm to the
towering arch of another mountain, its tip thrust heavenward
against the dazzling blue sky. Vicki took a deep breath of
the sweet, clear air that carried the scent of the wild flowers
covering the hillside.

There was another scent, too—something that was
strangely Ohio-familiar. Ah yes. There below her was a
large barn. Near it a dozen or so cows grazed in the lush
grass. She smiled, suddenly feeling more at home. There
was something universal about cows.

"Vicki?" Joe was touching her elbow, smiling down at
her, his face aglow with pleasure. "It's really something,
isn't it?"

"Oh, Joe, it's indescribable."

"Come." Anton was leading the way up the stone walk
to the front door. "We go inside and settle you, then give
the tour, yes?"

The moment they stepped inside the entrance hall, Joe
exclaimed, "Wow!"

"Ditto." Vicki stared around her in open-mouthed ad-
miration. The front hall alone looked larger than the entire
Cambridge apartment. To the left of the door was a floor-
to-ceiling stained-glass window, and to the right stood a
life-sized marble sculpture of a little girl holding a kitten.
On the wall straight ahead hung a gilt-framed oil painting.
Vicki had some trouble with history, geography, and languages, but along with her own field of psychology, she
was very knowledgeable about music and art. That painting
was a genuine Degas or she'd eat it, frame and all.

"Father," Gretchen said, "I would like to go in and call
Conrad while you take Josef and Victoria upstairs."

"Fine."

There seemed to be constraint, stiffness, between father
and daughter. Vicki remembered Rudolph's words that hinted
at a need for improvement in that relationship.

She followed Anton up a flight of stairs that led out of
the entryway. The steps were dark wood, highly polished,
with a pale rose and beige Oriental runner held in place by

heavy brass rods secured in the crook of each step. The style of the rounded brass handrail matched that of the rods. Vicki ran her hand along it. It was so smooth it almost felt soft. At the top of the stairs was a small landing with a fringed rug that matched the runner. Straight ahead was a single door. On either side were recessed alcoves that held exquisite porcelain Madonnas.

Anton swung the door open and stepped aside for them to enter. Vicki and Joe walked in and almost bumped into each other as they stared around them, both too over-whelmed to say anything at first. Vicki finally found her voice. "Uncle Anton, how perfectly gorgeous!"

Anton looked puzzled. "Gorgeous?" There was a quick exchange in German between him and Joe; then his lips curved in a smile. "Ah! Gorgeous. Like beauty, yes?"

Vicki tried to close her mouth while she nodded.

"Yes, is beauty. This I like. Is good feel of outside, yes?"

"Oh, yes."

The entire upstairs was one living area, like a house on top of a house. It was so sun-swathed it gave the immediate impression of being a sheltered section of the outdoors. She made a complete turn. "Is all this for us?"

"Yes." Anton fairly beamed. "It is—what you say?—your compartment."

Vicki and Joe exchanged winks.

"I will put the suitcases in the bedroom. You and Josef, you wash up, rest. I see you below in one hour for the dinner? Is enough time?"

"Yes, certainly, plenty." Her words were stumbling out over each other. As soon as the door closed behind him, Vicki began to jump up and down in a circle around Joe. "Joe, Joe, Joe!" she gurgled. "Look at this! We've been whisked away on a magic carpet to never-never land! Have you ever seen anything like this in your whole, entire life?"

Joe looked awestruck. "I thought places like this only existed in *Architectural Digest*. Vicki, look at those sky-lights. There are four of them in this one room. I've always wanted a house with skylights. If Anton wants to keep us, as Dad said, maybe we should stay."

"Hmm." Vicki wandered through the huge open room. It included a living room, dining alcove, and a full-sized kitchen separated from the living space by a U-shaped counter. "It's an idea, but it would be one heck of a commute to work."

Both the wall-to-wall carpet and the walls were the color of golden sand, and the luxurious couch and three matching chairs were off-white. There were red accents in the area rugs, throw pillows, and dining chair seats.

"You realize, my love, that there is nothing phony in this place—I'd be willing to bet on it. The furniture is antique, the paintings are originals, and I have a feeling we shouldn't knock any of the pottery off the tables."

"Isn't this great?" Joe pushed open one of the double sliding glass doors and stepped out onto the balcony. Vicki joined him, and they stood, arms around each other, staring in awe at the Austrian Alps that towered in the distance.

She grabbed his hand. "Let's go look at the kitchen!" Pulling Joe along with her, she went to examine the ultra-modern cooking space. "This place has everything! Not only all the usual equipment, but look at this! A slicer and a juicer and a pasta maker, and a—" She stopped. "I don't know what this is. Maybe it sings to you while you prepare dinner. Do people this rich really cook? I think I'd just go out for dinner every night and let someone else do all the work."

"Oh, that'd get tiresome. We'd want intimate, candlelit suppers and intimate little breakfasts on the balcony."

"How about having a cook?"

"As long as she went home before we got intimate."

She stood thoughtfully, as though considering the idea. "Okay, I'll compromise. The cook can go home before dinner as long as you help with the dishes."

"I always help with the dishes. Let's go see what the bedroom looks like."

Full of the heady exuberance brought on by their plush surroundings, they went to the door Anton had gone through.

The bedroom, too, was enormous, and it continued the same color scheme. It also had sliding glass doors that led to its own balcony.

"Wow," Vicki exhaled, "it's like hovering over paradise in a luxurious balloon."

"Vicki, Vicki, will you look at this bed? And I'll bet this place is built so nothing can be heard downstairs!"

She laughed. "I can tell you've had a few days' rest; your ever-lustful thought patterns are back in full swing." She bounced on the edge of the oversized bed. "Nice springs. And what a gorgeous quilt. It has to be handmade." But Joe had gone through yet another door.

"Hey, hey, hey!" She followed his shout into a marvel in marble. Joe turned to look at her, a suggestive leer on his handsome face. "If I'm not mistaken, what we have here in this corner is an honest-to-God Jacuzzi. Vicki! This is our chance to try making love in one. I've always wondered if that was really possible."

She laughed. "I'm willing to give it a try, but not now. We've got less than an hour, and I'll be darned if I'll appear at your uncle's dinner table half dressed."

"Well, then, check out this shower. It has nozzles coming from every direction."

"Joe, I hate to squash any of your romantic notions, but sex in a shower isn't all that comfortable."

"In that case, says he, never to be deterred, dig this thick, soft, wall-to-wall carpet. How about—"

"Good grief! You're developing a bathroom fixation at the tender age of twenty-seven. You'll be a real pervert by the time you're a dirty old man."

"Good, that gives me something to look forward to. I want to drop dead of a heart seizure while pursuing you across our richly carpeted floor at the age of ninety-nine. Right after I've had you in the bed, of course."

"Much as I hate to postpone this sexual rampage, we'd better get cracking. Why don't you take a shower while I unpack something to wear? And leave the water running; this will have to be fast."

"Yeah, you're right."

He reached in to turn on the water. Vicki hesitated at the door. "Joe?"

"Hmm?"

"This may be crazy, but I get the funniest feeling that there's more to all this than an extravagant graduation gift and a desire on your uncle's part to get to know us."

Joe looked at her thoughtfully. "You know, I'm picking up the same signals. Well, we're probably about to find out." With that he began to undress for the shower.

When they arrived downstairs, Gretchen opened the door and ushered them into the living room. "I'd like you to meet my husband, Conrad. Conrad, this is my cousin, Joe, and his wife, Victoria."

Vicki forced herself to concentrate on the slim, nice-looking man and not allow her gaze to creep around her lush surroundings. "How do you do." She took Conrad's hand. "I'd like it if both you and Gretchen would call me Vicki."

"I am glad to meet you, Vicki." He seemed friendly and interested, emitting none of his wife's negative overtones.

While Joe shook hands, Vicki slowly looked around her. Nothing in her past could have prepared her for this. She was hemmed in by elegance.

Anton entered, carrying a tray of glasses. "Ah, you are here! Welcome to my home."

"Thank you. You mentioned a tour earlier. Is it considered impolite in Austria to request one?" Vicki asked hopefully.

"It would be my delight. Come." He led them through one breathtaking room after another. This lower floor was far larger than the upper, more than a full house in itself. The darkness of the wood paneling and the rich colors of the upholstery were offset by the waning daylight that poured through a wall of glass at the end of the living room.

"It's so beautiful," Vicki breathed. "Even the floor is a work of art."

"Yes, you are correct." Anton looked down at the intricately designed parquet floor. "It is done by a local crafts-man. The rugs are typical of their countries. Mexico, China, Egypt, Venezuela."

"And your paintings! How did you find them all? A collection like this must be incredibly difficult to acquire." She refrained from mentioning the cost.

Anton's eyes sparkled with pleasure. "You know the art! Then you and I we will study each one when the sun it is out more brightly. You will see in the Chagall the . . . ah, the texture!" He looked pleased with himself for finding the word. "It is my passion, the art. Are you liking my home?"

She smiled at him. There was an eager little-boy quality about his question. He was not so scary, this corporate giant. "I am loving your home. It is . . . *herrlich.*"

He chuckled. "Ah, Josef, already Vicki picks up the German!"

"Speaking of German, what's the word for *home?*"

"Heim."

"Heim. That's pretty easy." As Anton preceded them through the kitchen door she whispered to Joe, "What's the word for *museum?*"

"Shhh."

The kitchen was designed more for function than beauty. When Anton introduced them to the cook, Joe's laughing eyes met hers.

As they left the room, Joe dropped back by her side and whispered, "He can afford to have a cook; he's not married."

"What does that have to do with it?"

"She won't interrupt any intimate moments."

"Hey, just because he's single doesn't necessarily mean he's celibate."

Anton was well ahead of them in the hall, but Joe still kept his voice low. "What do you think? Like this place?"

"Oh, I don't know. I think he's overdone the Roman section a bit. An eighteen-hundred-year-old bust of Hercules on a marble pedestal is a touch ostentatious."

"Poor Uncle Anton. I wonder if he's noticed that Hercules is broken. One of his ears is missing."

"Well, he can probably get some stonemason to come in and replace it."

Hand in hand, they walked in to join the others.

Anton stood by a sideboard that held two bottles of wine. "And now we have the refreshment. We have a good red or the fine white as well."

Vicki looked at the "good red" and gulped. The label said Rothschild. "I'll have the red, please." She ignored Joe's surprised look. So she didn't like red wine much, but when else would she ever get a chance to drink a Rothschild?

"And now." Anton filled the glasses and passed them around. "While we are only the family, we drink to Josef and to Victoria."

So there *were* others coming. Vicki had noticed eight places set at the dining room table. Conrad was raising his glass to them, smiling; Anton was beaming with pleasure; and Gretchen was visibly struggling to look cordial. They echoed Anton's "Welcome" and drank.

The three others arrived a short time later. Herr and Frau Berchtold, and Herr Hollweg. Both men worked for Anton, and they shared an easy rapport with him that almost, but not quite, included Gretchen.

The meal was delicious: tender veal served with a light cream sauce, fresh asparagus, and a dessert of apple tarts and heavy cream. Vicki vowed, as she gobbled down every morsel, that she'd cut down on her intake at the next meal.

"And where do you live, Mrs. Beck? Anton has told me, but it is gone from my mind." Herr Hollweg, a rotund, balding man with twinkling gray eyes and a sunny smile, was observing her with interest.

"We live in Cambridge, Massachusetts. It's part of Boston."

"Ah, yes, Boston. I have been there on the business. It is a good city, Boston."

"Yes, wonderful. I grew up in Ohio, but Joe was raised in the Boston area. I went to college there and have worked there since. Joe and I both love it and want to stay."

"Yes? But maybe you change your mind. Austria is a nice place to live."

Vicki smiled, glancing around. "I agree, especially if you can live in a house like this."

Herr Hollweg laughed. "Yes. You see, already you discover the . . ." He had a habit of waving his fingers back and forth when he was searching for a word, as though they could catch it in midair and pop it into his mouth. He found it. "Advantage, yes? You find the advantage."

She took a sip of her wine and shook her head. "The 'advantage' in this case happens to belong to Uncle Anton. In fact, I'd say that Uncle Anton has just about *every* advantage."

"But Anton, he is missing one thing. He has not the son."

Vicki stared at him, her smile fading. "But Anton has a daughter."

"Ah. Daughter, yes. A beautiful daughter. But not the son."

Everyone had lapsed into German, and Herr Hollweg turned to answer a question, so Vicki took the chance to ponder his statement. *Anton has not the son.* Anton had brought them there at no small expense for reasons that seemed surface-clear but had distinct undercurrents. Gretchen resented their presence, and now Herr Hollweg had dropped a hint about their living in Austria.

Now come on, Vicki, she inwardly warned herself, don't create plots. But several things began to fall into place in her mind. Anton owned one of the largest metals-distribution businesses in the world. He had been instrumental in getting Joe the job he'd held for three and a half years before he returned to school, a job that just happened to be with a metals-distribution company in the United States. Two plus two equals . . . ?

Her eyes moved to Joe, and her musing mind snapped into total concentration. Joe, his beautiful blue gaze fastened on his uncle's face, was leaning forward, totally absorbed. He looked excited, and he kept nodding, obviously making brief, affirmative answers to whatever questions Anton was asking.

Vicki suddenly felt very cold. She had the sensation of

being on the outside looking in at this convivial group—
this convivial group that included her husband. *Joe,* she
suddenly longed to shout, *Joe, let's go home!* She closed
her eyes briefly, ordering herself to snap out of it. When
her eyes opened, Anton was standing, his friendly smile
shedding warmth on his guests, suggesting that they move
to the living room for a schnapps.

By the time the evening had ended and Vicki and Joe
were climbing the stairs to their rooms, she was feeling the
weight of the accumulated hours since they'd left Massachusetts the night before. They'd packed the last of their
gear, been driven to the airport by a friend, flown to Zurich,
losing six hours in transit, laid over there, then flown on to
Salzburg, met a whole new group of people, stepped from
one culture to another and from near-poverty to opulent
luxury, and struggled with a language barrier.

Her fatigue, she thought, was understandable. What
wasn't understandable was why Joe was all but dancing up
the stairs. His eyes were sparkling even beyond their usual
brightness, reminding her of an old advertising slogan. What
was it? Oh, yes: snap, crackle, and pop.

"What is it with you?" she asked. "Are you on a graduation high?"

The blue eyes flicked to hers, their light near blinding.
"Me?"

She stopped, casting an exaggerated look around. "Well,
I don't see anyone else in the hall."

"Why? Am I acting any different?"

"You're all but crackling with energy. You're acting a
lot more like someone who's just had a three-week vacation
lying on a beach than someone who's put in three years of
almost continuous sixteen-hour days."

"All that ended five whole days ago."

"Well, I, for one, am ready to pitch over."

Joe swung their door open. "Would you look at that?
There's even a light that goes on automatically when you
open the door!"

"The wonders of wealth. I think I could get used to this."

"Could you really?"

She stared at him. "Well, of course I could really. Who couldn't? There aren't too many people around who aspire to being poor. But rich? That's another matter."

"Do you like Austria?"

She switched on the bedroom light, then turned to observe him with a puzzled frown. "The section of Austria that lies between the airport and here looks great. What is this, Joe?"

Joe regarded her thoughtfully, his eyelids half closed in speculation, then shrugged. "Nothing. Now that you mention it, I'm tired, too. I suggest we find out what the bed feels like."

Her eyes narrowed. "I have a feeling you're hiding something, Josef Beck, but I'm too tired to pursue it. I've got to crash."

Vicki was forcing herself up out of a deep, dark pit. A very comfortable deep, dark pit. One part of her sleep-sodden mind urged her to resist the compulsion to wake up and simply to fall back onto that soft, cushiony pad at the pit bottom. But some obnoxious little brain cell was nagging, tugging her unwillingly toward the dim, faraway light of wakefulness. She opened her eyes.

No wonder she couldn't sleep! The full moon flooded the room, while millions of stars twinkled at her through the skylights.

She turned onto her side and immediately became aware of Joe, sitting bolt upright on the other side of the enormous bed. He had several pillows propped behind him, and he was simply sitting there, staring off into some mysterious space. She had never seen him do this before. It was somehow frightening.

"Joe?" No response. Her heart skipped. "Joe!"

"What...what? Oh...Vicki. Hi, hon. What are you doing awake?"

"What am *I* doing? I just happened to wake up, probably because this is a little like sleeping in the middle of a lighting-fixtures store. Darling, why are you sitting there wide awake in the dark?"

She could see the flash of his teeth. "If I'm not mistaken, you just said it wasn't dark in here."

"You know what I mean!"

"Yes, I know what you mean." He pulled the extra pillows from behind his back and scooted over, sliding down beside her to gather her into his arms. "You mean, why was I sitting up, wide awake?"

"That's it."

"I don't know. I just couldn't sleep."

"But why didn't you go to the other room and read or something?"

"All the books around here are in German."

"You read German."

"Right, I forgot." He hugged her closer. "How about making love?"

"Joe! Stop changing the subject!"

"Who's changing the subject? The truth is that I was trying to be nice and not wake you. I was sitting there with my eyes wide open because my skin is stretched so tight I can't close them, all due, in case you haven't noticed, to the"—Vicki put her hand across his mouth, and he pulled it away—"I have."

"Josef—" Before she could say anything else he covered her mouth with his.

He raised his head to look at her, the moon lighting his handsome face, which was suddenly very serious. "I need you, honey. I need to make love with you." His mouth took hers again with a near ferocity, his arms holding her as though she were trying to escape.

He slid down and took one of her nipples in his lips, sucking on it gently, pulling it into his mouth, then pushing it out with his tongue. His forefinger was moving around her other nipple in tiny teasing circles.

Vicki felt something waking up deep inside. "Oh, Joe," she murmured. Her breasts were sending tingling sensations up to prick her body and mind into full awareness.

Joe slid up to kiss each side of her mouth. "I think you're waking up," he teased.

"You're an awful blabbermouth," she whispered. "Why don't you be quiet and kiss me?" He did. She was sure she could feel his dimple in his kiss, that one touch of visual softness creeping into tactile form, making his firm lips meltingly tender and pliable.

"I love the taste of your lips," he murmured. "In fact, I love the taste of every part of you." He licked the hollow at the base of her neck, then nibbled his way back to her breast, licking the taut tip, pressing it with his soft lips. There was no longer a sleeping molecule in her body. Mmm, Joe knew how to do such lovely things with his tongue. She knew just where she'd like to feel it right now.

Even as she had the thought he was moving that tantalizing tongue tip to another location. Oh, that felt wonderful. Desire for sleep was banished, replaced by a throbbing desire for more, more of this incredible pleasure. She lay very still in order to feel each and every exquisite sensation. The tongue had become titillator, torturer, teaser, slipping back and forth over the core of her awakened senses.

His arms stretched out, elbows hugging her waist, palms cupping her swelling bosom, long fingers rubbing the passion-hard tips. Oh, she willed, let his tongue never tire and his fingers never stop. She opened her eyes, aware that the brilliant moonlight contributed to the sensual aura, the stars beckoning, cajoling her to skyrocket up to join them in the ether of space. She felt as if she was blazing into a red-hot star, lifted by heat waves into the astral company of those other fiery denizens of the superstrata. "Joe!" She was ready to soar. "Joe, come with me!"

He slid up and into her, igniting her senses, sending the rocket into the atmosphere. Vicki felt she was exploding into millions of tiny particles of vibrating ecstasy, her head thrown back, her legs wound tightly around her precious tormentor, her arms flung wide on the bed in delicious abandon.

Slowly, slowly the pieces settled back into her one body,

peaceful now, sated now, sleepy once again.

She was dropping swiftly toward that warm, cuddly cushion at the bottom of the welcoming pit. From far, far away she heard . . . "Vicki?"

"Mmm, what?" Had she spoken out loud? She didn't know.

"Anton has offered me a job."

"What?" She wished the voice would stop. The soft cushion beckoned.

"How would you like to live here in Salzburg?"

"I can't live in Salzburg. I'm an American." She didn't think any sound had come out. But then, this was just a dream.

"It's a fantastic opportunity."

"I want to go home, Joe."

"Poor baby, you're sound asleep, aren't you? You can't even hear me. I'll tell you about it tomorrow." Silence, blessed silence. Then, still farther away, "It's an incredible opportunity. I'd be second in command . . . all that power."

He was talking to himself now, but she could hear him in her dream. An old quotation, something she'd read somewhere . . . Two things excite a man: sex and power. Silly dream. Joe had never been interested in power. Besides, he was an American, too. I want to go home now. Suddenly the pit was no longer friendly, but bottomless and menacing. How could she get out of it? You'll never get out, you'll never get out, you'll nev . . .

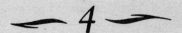

WHEN VICKI AWOKE, the room was again ablaze with light, but this time it was brilliant sunshine. It was really very pleasant, this sensation of living outdoors. Speaking of pleasant... She looked over at her sleeping husband, remembering their wonderful lovemaking during the night. There was something else about last night... Her eye caught the bedside clock. Ye gods! Eight-thirty, and they were due downstairs for breakfast at nine.

She nudged Joe, who was lying on his back with a pillow over his face. "Honey, wake up."

"Don't punch me," he mumbled into the pillow. "I'm dead."

"How dead?" She took hold of a few of the hairs on his chest and yanked.

"Ouch!"

"Not very," she answered herself. "Come on, sleeping beasty, we have to be downstairs in about twenty minutes."

"Oh, hell. Rush, rush, rush. Life is one long—" He took the pillow off his face and sat up. "Anton. We're having breakfast with Anton."

"Yes."

She almost got squashed by his speedy exit toward the bathroom.

"So much for sweet nothings whispered in my ear about last night."

Vicki closely watched the two men all through breakfast, which was served on the lovely brick terrace under the shade of a leafy tree. Busy, dun-breasted robins pulled worms out of the slope in front of them. She wondered why their coloring was different. Maybe the red-breasted robins lived down the road in Russia.

"So, today we have the program." Anton turned his considerable charm on her. "Gretchen comes to take you both on a tour of Salzburg, and I stay and work with all the papers."

"That sounds like a delightful program for us and a not-so-delightful program for you." She had noticed all through breakfast that Anton seemed distracted, and that he and Joe had a brief exchange in German before they sat down. There was something . . . If only she could remember.

"Salzburg I know like this"—he tapped the back of his hand—"but I do not speak to you well the history like my Gretchen. She speaks your language well, yes?"

"Very well."

"Good. Then she will come to your door at eleven. You have the tour and lunch. I see you here at six in the evening."

When they got back upstairs, Vicki kicked off her shoes and settled into one of the cushiony chairs near the sliding glass door. Cushiony. What did that make her think of? That dream last night, the one that kept creeping to the edge of her mind . . .

"Vicki?"

"Oh! I didn't see you there." Joe sat down in the chair opposite her.

"That's because you were off in another world." He ran a finger up and down the arm of the chair, his expression thoughtful. "Honey, I have something to talk to you about."

"Okay."

"It's important."

"All right, I'm paying attention."

Joe smiled at her, running his finger nervously up and down the chair arm once again. "I guess I'm a little anxious about this."

Vicki frowned. "Is something wrong?"

"Oh, no! Quite the opposite. Everything may be more right than I ever dreamed possible."

"Joe, what is it? I'm dying of curiosity."

"Well . . . Anton has offered me a job."

Vicki gasped. "So it wasn't a dream."

"What do you mean?"

"You told me this last night, didn't you?"

"Yes, but I thought you were asleep and didn't hear me."

"So did I."

"What?"

"Nothing. I'm sorry . . . It's so confusing. I thought it was a dream." She stared at him, her eyes widening. "Did you also say something about our living here in Austria?"

"Yes." His face was alight with excitement. "Anton says that he's fifty-nine years old and he'd like to retire in five or six years." Joe was now sitting on the edge of the chair, his elbows on his knees, his body bent forward in a position of tense anticipation. "Vicki, he wants me to learn the business so I'll be ready to take over. I'd be president of Beck Metals Corporation! Do you know what that means? We'd be rich enough to afford all this"—his hand waved around— "and more! Vicki, it's more than the chance of a lifetime. It's the end of the rainbow!"

Vicki was stunned. Joe was right; it was an incredible offer. So why did she feel so frightened? "But, Joe, how could we do it? I mean, living in a foreign country for a year, even several years, is one thing. But, I don't know, the idea of living permanently outside my own country . . . the concept is stupefying."

"It's a lot to grasp at first. That's why he wanted us to come here now, and again at the end of our trip to Switzerland. He thought we could discuss it while we relaxed."

"Why do I have the feeling that this is going to cut into the relaxation considerably?" She stood and walked to the glass door, sliding it open so she could step out onto the balcony. "The whole idea is overwhelming. I feel as if I just walked into a thick fog."

He came up behind her and wrapped his arms around her waist. "I know, hon. It's hard to believe. I'd always assumed I'd start at the bottom of the management ladder in some company and spend the next twenty years working my way slowly up, step by step. Here I'd be starting practically at the top of the ladder and zipping up to the tip of the extension. This is real stratosphere stuff, honey."

Stratosphere. A far different stratosphere from the one she'd visited the night before. "We really would be rich, wouldn't we?" A few bubbles of excitement began to rise inside her.

"Very. I could finally give you all the things I've wanted you to have. You could start your own art collection, and you could travel, and—"

"What's all this *you?* What happened to *we?*"

"Well, I'd be on a tough schedule for a few years. There's a lot to learn."

She turned and slid her arms around his waist, resting her cheek on his broad chest. "I was hoping we'd have more time together now that you're out of school."

"But don't you see, hon?" He took hold of her shoulders, staring into her eyes with his uniquely concentrated focus. "It would be worth the sacrifice for a while. Just think of the gain!"

She felt a strange mixture of exhilaration and anxiety. Maybe it was just too good to be true. She remembered the excitement of Joe and Anton at the table the night before. No wonder they'd looked so involved. And of course Herr Hollweg's remark... Then she remembered another picture: Gretchen listening to her father and the stranger who was her cousin, a look of anger and anguish on her face. Suddenly, inexplicably, Vicki felt a wave of fear. This whole "vacation" was assuming new, troubling proportions.

"Vicki, honey." Joe was stroking her hair. "There's no sense in our trying to sort this out now. It's all too new. We need some time to think about it. Although, I must admit, at the moment it's hard for me to see a lot of negatives."

"Joe, what would *I* do?"

"What do you mean?"

"Day after day, what would I do?"

He stared at her, dumbfounded. It was crystal clear he hadn't even thought about it. "Well, gosh, hon. We could start our family. There sure wouldn't be any need for you to work."

"You know I work because I want to as well, and I have no wish to stop working. I'm very good at what I do."

"Well, maybe you could get a job here."

"How? It would take me ages to learn to speak German well enough even to carry on a conversation. My work entails counseling troubled children. To do that I have to know a language inside and out, all the subtleties and nuances and slang expressions, so I can grasp the children's deepest thoughts and feelings. I can't imagine *ever* doing that in German."

Joe was beginning to show signs of impatience. "Vicki, you've wanted to go back to school. I'm sure there are universities with classes in English. Giving up your job might be a problem for a time, but nobody can have everything."

A creeping chill invaded her heart. *But you can, Joe. You're being offered everything.* She didn't say it because even the thought made her feel mean and ungrateful. Anton *was* offering them a chance to live in a manner beyond their wildest dreams. She had to admit it was immensely compelling.

The doorbell rang. Gretchen was here. Vicki turned abruptly to Joe. "What about Gretchen?"

"That must be her at the door."

"That's not what I mean. How does she fit into this— this power structure?"

Joe looked harassed. "That's not my business, Vicki.

That's Anton's decision. I'm sure something would be worked out."

Vicki looked at him for a moment. Was Joe changing, or was she imagining things? "You'd better open the door."

Joe swung the door open and met the cool, level gaze of his cousin Gretchen. Everything about Gretchen seemed cool and rigidly controlled, an impression that was enhanced by the severe cut of her dark hair, and the trim, tailored cut of her gray suit with its accompanying starched white shirt and black string tie. Her large hazel eyes seemed devoid of expression.

"Good morning, Josef. Are you and Victoria ready to depart?"

"Yes. Please come in while I grab a jacket. Do I need a tie for any reason?"

"No. A tie is not necessary."

Joe walked to the chair where he had draped his sports jacket as Vicki went to greet Gretchen. What was it about Gretchen that bugged him so? Certainly not her looks. She was really quite lovely, if you could ignore the coating of ice. A little mind-devil nagged that he knew what the problem was, but he shut the door on that notion. "Okay, all set."

There was no question about who would take the wheel. Gretchen automatically slid into the driver's seat, letting Joe and Vicki decide who would sit where in the red Volkswagen. Vicki insisted on crawling into the back seat, reminding Joe that he needed room for his long legs. He was grateful for the space, but not so grateful to be in the line of fire of Gretchen's conversation.

He needn't have worried. She didn't speak to them until they got to Salzburg, except to remind them to produce their passports for the double border crossings.

The drive took less than thirty minutes, and they were soon entering a parking garage that appeared to have been cut into the mountain. It was. The moment the car was parked, Gretchen began to talk in a flat, tour-guide voice.

"This garage is built since the war. It is intended to be

used as a shelter, in case there is again such a need. As they walked out into the sunlight, she continued, "There you see the watering trough built for the archbishop's horses. Behind the statue are frescoes of prancing stallions. The horse has always been much revered in Salzburg."

Joe felt a bit like a schoolboy following his teacher. Vicki, with clear intent, trailed behind. Being a history buff, Joe was intensely interested in this city that was so closely tied to the fortunes of his ancestors, and he resented Gretchen's cold, disinterested manner.

He walked along, too lost in thought to concentrate on Gretchen's continuing narrative, absorbing his own impressions of the tidy, bustling city with its unmistakable air of antiquity. Antiquity, beauty, and friendliness. People smiling, in the middle of a city! Then the sound of Vicki's hushed tone brought his attention back to his companions.

"Oh, Joe, can you believe how incredibly beautiful this is?"

As he looked left, right, and around, something began to swell in his heart, some indefinable pride of identification in the sheer magnificence of his surroundings. His surroundings. His Austrian surroundings. He began to concentrate on what Gretchen was saying.

"You are in the Domplatz. As you see, it is built in a square, the buildings facing the courtyard. In the sixteenth century, Archbishop Wolf Dietrich, who had decided that the city was crowded and disagreeable, had this section razed. He then had new plans laid, fashioned after his beloved Florence."

As Gretchen spoke, Joe silently studied her. Her gaze traveled around the square, and a spark began to kindle in the depths of her hazel eyes. She loves this place, he realized. The pride he was just getting a taste of was magnified in her a thousandfold. "You love Salzburg, don't you."

Her eyes, now aglow, met his. "Yes, I love Salzburg. To me it is the heart of Austria. It is a city for Austrians." Their eyes locked, the challenge clear. *A city for Austrians, and you are not one of us.*

Joe let his gaze drop, not eager for a confrontation with his cousin. He could see the anxiety in Vicki's glance, could almost hear her plea to go slowly. He gave her a reassuring smile. All he really wanted at this moment was to absorb the wonder that surrounded him. "Gretchen, beauty of this magnitude has universal appeal. Even uncouth Americans can appreciate it." He couched the gentle reprimand in a teasing tone, a quietly offered peace treaty.

The spark in Gretchen's hazel eyes flared momentarily, then settled into a warmer sheen, and the corners of her mouth turned up ever so slightly. "You are right, of course. My apologies. And Americans are not uncouth. Americans have been to us very good friends. Come, we will savor this feast together."

The relief on Vicki's face was so evident that Joe couldn't repress a wink in her direction. The air between the three of them now only slightly less clear than the air around them, they walked to the center of the large square.

Joe listened to Gretchen. Her voice began to take on inflections and warmth as she seemed to forget them in her increasingly impassioned description.

"Here in this square is where the Salzburg music festival begins, usually in the last week of July. As you see, the great fortress, sitting as it does five hundred feet above the city on that massive mountain, forms the perfect backdrop. At night, during the festival, the fortress is floodlighted from the other end of the Mönchsberg on the right bank of the Salzach, the river. Stand just so"—she faced them in the direction of the towering fortress, a mighty monument to yesteryear's grandeur—"and picture the huge square, crowded with people, most of them in evening dress, hushed and reverent, waiting for the spectacle to begin.

"There on the steps of the cathedral, in front of the three doors that are carved to represent Faith, Hope, and Charity, are gathered hundreds of performers—the symphony orchestra, the opera singers, the chamber musicians—all of whom will disperse to the various halls later for their first concerts. The caller announces that the festival has begun.

The trumpeter, who stands up there on the parapet, sounds the call, and all the musicians and singers join in a mighty musical chorus that shakes the heavens and stirs the heart." She stopped, as though embarrassed by her effusiveness.

"Why, Gretchen." Vicki stepped to her side, touching her arm. "That paints such a clear, eloquent picture. How kind of you to share your vision of that with us."

Gretchen's face was a study in contrasts. Joe watched, fascinated. Gretchen was in imminent danger of liking Vicki, he realized. But then, no one could resist Vicki for long.

Gretchen blinked, then tilted her head back, as though collecting her thoughts. When she spoke, there was a trace of warmth in her tone. "Thank you, Vicki. It is a sight that is without parallel. You must come to visit us at that time."

It's a great place to visit, but don't plan to live here, Joe mentally finished for her.

"The other great highlight," she continued, "is a play—Hugo von Hofmannsthal's adaptation of *Everyman*. This morality play is presented at every festival. It is tradition."

Tradition. Joe's eyes wandered lovingly over the buildings he had heard and read so much about: the marble columns that fronted the cathedral; the fortress, which had sheltered so many generations of besieged townspeople and served a steady line of archbishops as their seat of power; glorious St. Peter's Church, built originally in the eighth century, then remodeled and added to throughout the ages in the varying architectural styles of the times, becoming a marvel of melded Romanesque, Gothic, baroque, and rococo.

"It is most funny," Gretchen said, clearly loosening up, "to hear at six every evening the lovely thirty-five-bell carillon of the Glockenspiel Tower, followed by the organ from the fortress, which has two hundred barrel pipes and sounds like a bull with a bad stomach."

Vicki laughed. "Can we stay for that?"

"I think father expects you back by six."

"Oh, yes, I forgot."

Gretchen, her ice shield defrosting, smiled at her. "But

we will make it the point to return and to hear the bull."
She took a quick peek at her watch. "Shall we have lunch?
Then you can decide if you wish to ride up the cog railway
to go through the fortress, or visit the birthplace of Mozart,
or"—the slightly timid smile flowered again—"so many
things to see. Perhaps you will want to visit an American
import."

"What's that?" Vicki was swinging along beside Gretchen,
all traces of tension gone.

"Come, I show you." They walked down a narrow street
of small shops, each with an elaborate scrolled metal sign
above the door indicating the type of business. She pointed
up at a fancy sign that, on close examination, revealed a
familiar form carefully hidden in the emblem. "You see,
they bow to Austrian reserve and modify the golden arch."

Joe laughed aloud, feeling completely at ease for the first
time. "Well, if you don't mind, no hamburgers for me,
please. Not in Salzburg."

Holding the tenuous threads of camaraderie tightly, they
entered a cozy little coffee house that looked as though it
hadn't changed for at least five hundred years.

Joe was terribly hungry and terribly confused. So much
to grapple with in so short a time. A part of him wished to
ignore the hurt look in his cousin's eyes, but his honest
nature, nudged by Vicki's prickly glances, was pushing him
toward broaching the subject that was on their minds.

He waited until they placed their orders, then jumped in.
"Gretchen," he began, "I think there's something we should
talk about."

An expression of panic crossed Gretchen's face. She took
a deep swallow of her water and slowly lifted her eyes to
his. "So. And what is it you wish to discuss?"

She wanted to avoid this as much as he did, he thought.
Maybe he should just tell her he wanted to see the Resi-
denzplatz after lunch, and let it go.

"Joe . . ."

As usual, Vicki seemed able to read his mind. At times
it was lovely, but at other times—like now, when his own

conscience was attempting to go on strike—it was very irritating. He sent her a contrite, I'll-be-good smile. "Obviously you're aware that Anton has asked me to join the firm." That was putting it as gently as he knew how.

"My father has not just asked you to join the firm; he has asked you take the position second only to his, in anticipation of becoming the president of the company when he retires." Not so gentle.

Vicki couldn't stay out of it. She leaned forward, her green eyes alight with concern. "How do you feel about it?"

Gretchen stared at her hands, which were clasped on the tabletop. "It is not my place to question his decisions. If that is his wish, then so be it."

Joe inwardly fumed. Dammit, this German reserve was sometimes a royal pain in the prat. Why didn't she just say how she felt, so they could discuss it? On the other hand, if she wanted to be stiff-necked about it, to hell with her. And what are you so sore about? his nosy conscience carped. Afraid she might really tell you how she feels?

Vicki studied Joe. He was hedging, and it worried her. He really wanted this position. She could read the hunger in his eyes. And that hunger was shutting out the needs of his "competition." She shivered, trying to push aside an uneasy thought. Could power be corrupting him already, before he even had it? Well, there was no way she was going to play this little game.

"Gretchen," she began, avoiding Joe's eyes, "we're both concerned about your part in this. I get the feeling that you're not entirely happy about the whole thing. And before Joe and I decide what we should do, we must know where you stand. After all, we'd be moving halfway around the world. It would help to know in advance how you feel."

The cheerfully bustling waitress placed steaming bowls of bean soup before them, an interruption, Vicki saw, that was welcomed by both of her table companions. You and your big mouth, Vicki, she chided herself. Your husband may strangle you when you get back to the apartment.

The silence grew heavy. Vicki tentatively tasted a spoonful of her soup. Ouch. Too hot. Just like the luncheon conversation.

And how do you like the idea of my darling husband moving in and wresting the control of that charming little business from you, Gretchen, my dear? says I.

Why, I think it's just ducky, answers she. I'd far rather sit home and raise babies, lots and lots of babies, maybe a dozen or so.

Now, isn't that keen, I reply keenly. It seems that we are both programmed for the same destiny. Ah, motherhood.

Vicki shook her head, angry at herself for her poor-me mental rumblings. She couldn't understand her own attitude. This was *her* chance of a lifetime, too. Why didn't she feel gratitude instead of this foolish, unwarranted anger? She was probably projecting her own American feminist attitude. Having babies and staying home to care for them might be exactly what Gretchen desired. But that brief thought was emphatically shattered.

Gretchen, her eyes fixed on her hands, which were now placed flat on either side of her bowl, began to speak, and this time she made no attempt to hide the bitterness in her tone. "You want to know how I feel? Then know. I am so angry it is making my insides roll up in tight balls. I have been the right-hand 'man' to my father for these six years. Everyone knows it. Herr Hollweg knows it. Herr Berchtold knows it. They know also that I am competent. I am like my father. The business, it comes to me naturally. I will have a family, yes. But the business, it is my first love, more than the babies, more than my husband, more than all but my father. For him is the highest love. And now, the highest hate. Does that shock you? My husband, he understands. He aches for my pain. He, too, has another love—the medicine."

Finally she looked up into their stunned faces. "It is not your fault, this I know. Papa will take the business from me because I am a woman and he still has the old-fashioned ideas. A woman will not—what is it you say?—stick it out. So now you have it, the way I feel."

Her palms had turned upward, almost visibly cupping her hurt. Joe stared at them, captured by the image of all that power slipping through her fingers... and into his.

He dropped his eyes, afraid she, or more significantly, Vicki, would see the avarice that must be gleaming there. What was happening to him? He never would have believed that greed could take such hold of him. Was it greed? Or simply the age-old urge to rise to a challenge, to conquer the world. He'd certainly never thought he'd have a crack at this much of it!

But Josef Anton Beck was a creature of his background and upbringing, and he couldn't sustain meanness for long. He felt his sensibilities returning. Taking a deep breath, he said, "I don't want to crowd you out, Gretchen." Her eyes met his. "I could work for you. It wouldn't offend me to report to a woman. After all, I've had lots of practice; I check in every morning to get my orders from Vicki." Vicki hooted, but to his dismay, he saw tears welling up in Gretchen's eyes.

"You are most kind, and you lighten my burden with your words. But you might as well accept what is being offered you, for there is one thing I cannot change, and that is my sex." At last, a full-fledged smile. "At least, that is too far to go, even for me. And now we must eat the soup before it gives us the frostbite. Then we go take a look at the Festspielhaus, where the walls have stored so much music that it oozes out to serenade you as you pass through."

As Gretchen turned her flustered attention to her lunch, Vicki reached over to take Joe's hand. "I love you," she mimed.

He got the message, and once again he thanked heaven Vicki was always there to help prod him back to humane concerns.

When they had finished lunch and were once again out on the busy street, Joe announced, "I know one thing I'd like to do. I'd like to buy some lederhosen. Now that I'm free of the pressures of academe, I plan to hit the mountain trails." He paused, glancing from one to the other. "I mean, either here *or* in the good old U.S., there are lots of trails just waiting."

Gretchen nodded. "I understand. The talk was good. We should not have between us the uneasiness. Now, we go to find the lederhosen."

After looking at hiking pants in three different stores, Joe threw up his hands in surrender. "Well, it's back to L. L. Bean for me. Those things are expensive! At that price I should be able to buy a mountain of my own!"

His cousin stopped to look at a particularly ornate pair of the leather walking shorts in a window. "You see, the embroidering is all hand done. And that is the quill of a bird feather stitched into place. The pants, they are made to last for a lifetime, and they are never washed."

Vicki clapped Joe on the arm. "That shoots it, my love. I've had more than one whiff of your clothes after just a one-weekend hike. If you bought a pair of those, they'd have to live outside!"

With exploring more treasures of art, architecture, and geography than could be properly viewed in a month, the day went all too quickly.

Vicki was particularly fascinated with the catacombs that were scraped into the Mönchsberg, a high ridge on the right bank of the Salzach. As they stooped over to make their way through the cramped corridors and into the small dug-out rooms, Gretchen happily satisfied Vicki's curiosity, telling her the history of the area and of the government's efforts to preserve what remained after a major landslide.

Vicki looked through a hole in the mountainside at the splendor of the city of Salzburg with its riotously beautiful architecture. "I love the combination of the rococo and the baroque. Those styles are so happy. So many little cherubs, all smiling, throwing flowers, or strumming lutes. It's especially nice to look down on it, since agony seems to be relegated to the lower statues."

Gretchen laughed delightedly. "Yes, you are right. And the buildings, they have been altered over the ages, so they now combine the changing styles of many centuries."

Joe stood close behind them, looking over their shoulders, enjoying, at least for the moment, their cozy companionship. "Salzburg is what I would call a successful amalgamation."

The word stumped Gretchen, so Joe explained its meaning as they carefully made their way down the steep, dark stairs.

When the time came for them to start back, Vicki again volunteered to take the back seat. Her eyes grabbed the scenic treats the car sped past: stacks of hay heaped to dry in mounds; fields of tall grass not yet cut; the ever-visible alpine mountains dominating the view; neat, quaint houses; neat roadways; neat sidewalks. If cleanliness was next to godliness, these people had a head start up the celestial ladder.

She tried very, very hard to imagine living here. She pretended she already did and was returning to her home after a day in the city. It didn't work. Just how did you turn a midwestern, America-first girl into an Austrian? she wondered.

They made it to Anton's door at precisely six o'clock, having almost run over each other to accomplish it. She wondered what would happen if they were a few minutes late. Maybe the little marble girl in the front hall would trip them, or perhaps her marble kitten would scratch them. She was amused, when they entered the foyer, to catch herself circumventing the statue.

Anton, in what seemed to be his permanent demeanor, showered them with jovial cheer. "You have the good tour?"

"Yes, indeed," Vicki assured him. "Gretchen is a superb guide. Her knowledge of history and art is staggering."

"Yes. A very smart woman, my Gretchen."

Then why don't you let her run your company, instead of making her feel so second-class? Slow down, she urged herself. Her feminist fangs were showing.

Anton supplied them each with a glass of yet another delicious wine, then sat beside Vicki on the sofa. "Louisa"—

Louisa was Anton's cook—"will serve us the light supper. It will be necessary for us to not take too much time. Today you have the touring program, and tonight you have the culture program."

"Oh?" Vicki hoped the alarm she felt didn't show on her face.

"Yes. I got for us the tickets to the Salzburger Schlosskonzert. They will have for us"—he consulted a slip of paper—"the evening of Mozart." He smiled at them. "Of course, always Mozart, and also Schubert and Elgar and Mendelssohn." He beamed. "Does that not sound nice?"

Joe tugged at his collar, his startled gaze glancing off Vicki's. "Y—yes, wonderful. Is the concert in Bad Reichenhall?"

"No, no. It is to be in the Residenz, in Salzburg."

Vicki refrained, just in time, from yelping, "Salzburg!" The touring program and the culture program. Whatever happened to the sleep program?

The concert was magnificent, Vicki thought later that night as she lay in bed curled tightly against her sleeping husband, just as the city was magnificent and this house in which they were guests was magnificent. And all of this magnificence was being offered to them on a solid gold platter. Why didn't the golden gleam seem more enticing?

The problem was, it was a long way from home. And there was no doubt in her mind about where home was. Home was America.

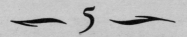

5

"I TOLD YOU it wouldn't work!"

"Now come on, Vicki, we haven't given it a fair shake yet."

"And just what, may I ask, is a fair shake? More to the point, *where* is a fair shake? I have yet to see a wobble, let alone a shake!"

"But I've read about this in a lot of books. There has to be a way..."

"Joe! I'm getting all puckered."

"Puckered, you say? Well, sweetie pie, it can only be one step from being puckered to being—"

"Josef Anton Beck, stop right there. In fact you can *stay* right there. But I'm getting out of this Jacuzzi. I can stand only so much hot whirling water. Besides, we're not getting anywhere. All in all, I vote for bathroom floors—if, that is, you're determined to pursue your bathroom fetish."

Vicki climbed out of the swirling water, feeling, she had to admit, thoroughly relaxed. No wonder Joe wasn't having any success. That hot water was enough to put you to sleep.

"Joe, seriously, you'd better get out of that tub before you liquefy and flow down the drain. Besides, I don't want to waste this precious by-ourselves day. Louisa must have been in here while we were gone yesterday. The refrigerator and the shelves are full of food. We could hole up here for a month! I'm going to make us one of those intimate breakfasts you seemed so fascinated by."

Joe grudgingly got out of the sunken tub and grabbed one of the thick, soft towels. He started to dry off, then stared down at himself in fascination. "Hey, honey, how do you like me like this? Kind of an interesting effect, don't you think?"

"Doesn't appeal to me. I've never cared for prunes."

"That's not very kind. Most of the prunes I've known have said nice things about you."

"The only thing any prune ever said to you was, 'Just passing through.'"

"Vicki, for the love of heaven, just go fix breakfast."

"No appreciation," she muttered as she went into the bedroom to dress, "for the fine art of levity."

"If that means you're about to ascend," Joe called, "be careful of the skylight!"

Vicki realized their good humor was magnified by the precious gift of this free day in which they could explore their grandiose surroundings by themselves. She hoped her enthusiasm hadn't been too obvious when Anton had apologetically explained that he must "go attend to the business."

She had a wonderful time making breakfast in the fully equipped kitchen. What a unique experience to put together a meal in a sparkly new kitchen with sparkly new utensils, she thought. She actually had no idea how old the apartment was, but it didn't look as if anyone had ever cooked a meal in there.

A little over an hour later, Joe was plaintively begging for his meal. When Vicki carried a laden tray to the balcony, he stared at it in wide-eyed astonishment. "I don't believe it."

"See? It wasn't my lack of culinary acumen at all, simply

the lack of every labor-saving device known to man, or in this case, woman." She watched proudly as Joe took the warm plates of eggs Benedict off the tray. "How about that? With uncurdled hollandaise sauce, yet!"

"I'm overwhelmed. And I thought we'd already reached the height of luxury." Taking a forkful, he purred, "Honey, this is delicious." He looked around. "Did you make coffee?"

"Right in front of you, in that thermos pitcher. We don't horse around with uninsulated containers in this household." She sampled the eggs. "Oh, hey, if I do say so myself, these are magnificent! Better than at the Ritz!"

"I'm sure that's true, although it's an unfair comparison. You probably didn't even taste the eggs at the Ritz. You ate them, but you didn't taste them."

"That's true. I was too excited by the prospect of this trip."

Joe looked at her thoughtfully. "Are you still excited?"

She poured them each a cup of steaming black coffee. "I'm still excited, but scared, too." She stopped eating for a moment to look intently at Joe. "Do you feel scared by all of this, or is it just me?"

He took a sip of coffee, then set the cup back on the china saucer, staring at it in deep contemplation. "I don't know. It still doesn't feel real enough, I guess. None of my everyday reactions are working. It's very disconcerting to have your dreams come true almost before you have time to dream them. I think I've always been ambitious, as well as determined. I'm sure all the stories of the fabulous uncle in Austria contributed to that ambition. I remember, even as a young boy, thinking that when I grew up I wanted people to talk about me the way they did about Anton. You know what I mean, Vicki; I'm sure you've heard it in my parents' voices, and those of their friends who know of Anton's achievements. It's a tone of near-reverence. Everyone seems to be awed by that degree of success. People are almost obsequious toward the rich and the powerful, and the combination of both . . ."

Joe's voice trailed off, and Vicki studied his expression closely. Before she could give form to the troubled feeling that welled inside her, Joe did it for her.

"Is it wrong, do you think, to be that ambitious?"

It took her a minute to reply. "I don't know how to answer that question. I guess if that kind of ambition didn't exist in the world, there'd be darned little progress, because it's probably the hunger for success that makes a person willing—even compels him—to devote a lifetime to hard work." She stopped, staring at him, startled. "Compulsion. You've used that word, haven't you, talking about yourself."

He nodded soberly. "Yes. I have it. The compulsion." He looked at her, his bright blue eyes troubled. "It frightens me a little, Vicki. It feels"—he gazed out over the sweeping vista of mountain peaks, hillsides covered with wild flowers amid waving grasses, and the bluest of skies—"sort of like a small creature living inside me, waiting to be fed, growing day by day." His eyes met hers. "There's no ignoring it, and no way to get rid of it. I sense that it will either force me to grow *with* it, in a healthy, creative manner, or it will outstrip me and consume me in the process."

Vicki stared down at the hollandaise sauce congealing on the uneaten portion of her egg. She took a sip of her coffee and leaned back, noting that a cloud had floated into view, marring the perfection of the sky. "Joe, doesn't it seem strange that Anton would make such an offer to you? I mean, you're his nephew, and of course *I* know you can do anything. But how much can he know about you? It seems inconceivable that a man who's spent his whole lifetime building a corporate empire would turn it over to some unknown young man just because he happens to have some of the same blood in his veins."

"He knows just about everything there is to know about me. He told me that in our first conversation. He knows what kind of a kid I was growing up, how my grades were all the way through school, what my work record was, how I did in graduate school, even how I'm regarded personally by teachers, other students, fellow workers, and close friends.

And believe me when I tell you he didn't get his information by asking my father!"

"But how . . . ?"

"Vicki, one thing money buys very, very easily is information. Especially readily available information. All he had to do was hire someone to ask the questions."

"Doesn't it offend you that someone was poking around and prying into our affairs?"

"Not at all. I'd do the same thing if I were considering making an offer like his."

"Joe! Dear God! He probably knows all about me, too!"

"Unquestionably."

Her hands dropped into her lap as she stared at him, dumbfounded. "I think . . . I think that *does* offend *me!*"

"I'm sorry."

I'm sorry, but you're part of the package and therefore must meet the specifications. No bizarre secrets to be hidden away, no aberrations allowed. It was the only time in her life she'd ever wanted any vices. She shook her head, trying to clear it. Now she was just being contrary. Joe was right, of course. Anton would have to check on them. He wasn't exactly offering a simple middle management position.

"Vicki?" Joe reached across the table to touch her arm. "Are you okay? You look kind of pale."

She felt kind of pale. She rubbed her eyes to dispel the strange film clouding her vision. "I'm all right, Joe. I just—" She stopped.

"No, no holding back. Say what you're thinking."

"It's silly."

"Say it anyway. We've never held back with each other."

"It's as if there's a little girl inside me saying, 'I want to go home now.' Isn't that foolish? I don't know why I should wish to run away, back to our shabby little retreat in downtown Cambridge. Because it isn't only your dream, you know. I've always wanted to live in luxury, too. Even growing up in fairly comfortable circumstances, you watch your parents do without things to save money to send all the kids to school, put off one bill so they can pay another, try to keep the old Chevy running for one more year, make do with the threadbare sofa to contribute to Grandma's heating bills. Sure, I've wanted to live in luxury, but my idea of luxury wasn't nearly this grand. Just being able to pay the bills the minute they come due, replace things as they wear out, buy new clothes now and then, get a new car before the old one has to be patched together with Scotch tape and prayer—that's luxury. I don't even know how to define the kind of lifestyle Anton has."

"You know how Anton describes his lifestyle?"

"No, how?"

"Simple. He told me that last night. He said, 'I have basically a simple life, Josef. I work, I have some time to come here to my beloved mountains, I share time with my daughter and Conrad and a few friends, most of whom I work with. My one hobby is collecting art, which I love to do.'"

Vicki put her elbow on the table, resisting the nagging need to glance around to be sure no one saw her do it, then leaned her chin on her hand. "From Anton's point of view, he's right. That's a pretty simple lifestyle. It's just a little more expensive than our simple lifestyle."

"You might say that. Well, my love, that was a repast fit for a king. Even a mighty management mogul. My thanks. I shall do the dishes. Fair is fair."

"Your mighty-mogul image is tarnishing already." They stood, both piling plates on the tray, and went to the kitchenette, where Joe insisted she stand back and let him do the work. Vicki watched him swish the water around the plates with the small round brush and stack them in the dishwasher. It was so familiar—this work-share program, as Anton would doubtless call it—so much a part of their three years together. How long would it take before the thought of helping with the dishes wouldn't even occur to Joe? Of course, she probably wouldn't have to do them either, if she chose not to.

Choices. Money also bought choices. She couldn't deny that she had a hunger for all of this, too. But...

"What are you thinking about?"

Joe's question caught her off guard. She hadn't realized

how far her mind had wandered. She didn't want to tell him, but they always shared everything: thoughts, feelings, hurts, triumphs. This was no time to start hiding things. "Joe, there's something growing in me, too. Not the way you described your compulsion, but very real just the same, and very insistent."

"Okay, shoot."

She pulled a chair over and sat carefully on the gold-embroidered red silk cushion. "It sounds corny and old-fashioned and outdated."

"Quit qualifying it, honey. If it's there, it's there. Just tell me."

"I suppose you'd call it patriotism, Joe. I'm a middle-class midwestern girl who was reared on the belief that there's no place in the world quite like the good old U.S. of A. And the funny thing is, I think I believe it. I just don't know if even for all this"—she waved her hand around—"I could leave my country, knowing that I wouldn't be coming back except as a visitor. I don't know, Joe. I just don't know if I could do it."

Their eyes met and held, because they both knew the size of the problem they faced if she couldn't. Then they silently returned to their chores.

When the dishes were done, the bed made, and the bathroom straightened—all of which felt like playing house in their plush surroundings—they decided that the best thing to do with their free day was spend it out-of-doors. Vicki began packing a lunch while Joe went down to the basement, where Anton had said there was a bit of hiking equipment. There was a closet *filled* with hiking supplies: backpacks, walking sticks, canteens, and all the other paraphernalia a true hiker accumulates. Ha! Joe thought. Uncle Anton clearly had at least one other hobby, because the things looked well used. He selected a small day pack and a canteen, then, after a brief inner debate, two of the fancier walking sticks. What the heck—might as well walk in style!

He stopped when he got back to the main floor, pausing in Anton's front hall, aware that he was testing the sensation of coming home to a house like this, one that belonged to

him. The pervasive silence was strangely reassuring, adding
to his fantasy of ownership. He glanced at the marble statue
of the young girl, at the lifelike kitten in her hand, at the
Degas painting and two small watercolors—Vicki had mentioned the artist, but he couldn't remember.

Taking his time, he wandered through the entire house,
squelching the breaking-and-entering feeling it gave him.
After all, Anton had told him to make himself at home in
his house, in his business, in his country. When he reached
the ancient bust of Hercules on its marble pedestal, he stopped
to run his fingers over the nicked features. "Sorry about the
ear, Herc old boy." But his attempt at levity did nothing to
halt the flood of wanting that came with the tour. How
wonderful to have an opportunity to own this kind of a
house, to be able, on a whim, to give Vicki a brand-new
kitchen or a bust dug out of a Roman ruin.

He went to the door of Anton's private study and paused.
Would this be real trespassing? He entered anyway, drawn
by the need to sit in Anton's chair. He sank slowly into the
rich brown leather, engulfed in a sense of power. From this
chair came multimillion-dollar decisions. Could he, Josef
Anton Beck, make decisions of that magnitude? Yes. There
was no doubt in his mind that he could, and he would love
it all: the discipline, the struggle, the intense work, and the
chance to achieve.

And what about Vicki? What if she didn't want to come
with him? He got up and headed slowly for the front hall,
taking a last look around. The silence hung more heavily.
It felt like loneliness now. Vicki had to come with him. She
just had to. He headed back upstairs, suddenly needing to
be near her.

In short order they had their gear packed and were walking through the fields, their hearts lightened by the glory of
the day. The air was crisp-apple fresh, scented by wild
geraniums and hill-hugging herbs.

"With my pack on my back and my love at my side,
I'll take hill and valley and mountain in stride."

Joe sang at full voice, his improvised lyrics sitting unsteadily on his improvised tune. He didn't care; he felt terrific. He stretched his legs out to full stride, swinging his arms and making up another stanza.

"With my heart pumping hard and my breath coming fast,
  I'll step to my future right out of my past!"

"Hey, that's pretty good! If all else fails, maybe you can become a songwriter." Vicki thought a moment, then added to the song:

"What a day to be young, what a day to be free,
  We're happy as songbirds, my lover and me.
  I will climb up the hills, I will stay by his side,
  If on the way back he will give me a ride!"

Joe reached out to grab her hand. "Fat chance, my lady. It's every man for himself. No! Don't say it. I'm fully aware that you're not a man."

They strode easily along for about two hours and trudged not so easily uphill for one. When they finally reached one of the jutting hillocks that offered the combination of a grassy knoll and a magnificent view, Vicki yelled, "Halt!"

Joe changed direction and returned to her side. "What's this 'halt' nonsense? Look up there." He gave a grandiose sweep of his arm. "There are higher peaks to climb, greater summits to scale!"

"Listen, Sir Edmund Hillary, you can work on scaling more peaks on your own time, without my feet next to yours. I'm tired and starving. Let's stop for lunch."

"Ordinarily I would resist your entreaties and push ahead, but if you're going to bring *food* into it . . . what do we have?" He unbuckled the backpack and set it on the ground.

Vicki loosened the strap and reached in to bring out the lunch, which she'd neatly packaged in plastic containers. "Are you ready for this? Not for us mere Wilson's meat bars or peanut butter sandwiches. We have, courtesy of our shadowy food-supply person, a lunch of cold sliced chicken, crabmeat salad, and cold white wine of a formidable vintage, all kept chilled by these nifty little frozen packets."

"Now really, what kind of provisions are those for a mountain man?"

"You don't want them?" She started to shove the food back into the pack.

"Hey! Don't be hasty. Since it's all you have, I'm willing to sacrifice and eat it. Just don't tell any of the other guys in the hill country."

"I promise."

His teasing jibes continued as she extracted a white linen tablecloth and silverware.

"Listen," she scolded, "don't give me a hard time. You're the one who got us into this weird place where they have no decent paper plates or plastic utensils. Is it my fault we have to suffer through this embarrassment of riches?"

High in location and spirit, they ate everything, including four small chocolates.

"Even the candy is gift-wrapped!" Joe popped his second one into his mouth and lay back on the lush grass.

Vicki carefully wrapped the plates and glasses in the cloth and napkins, repacked them, and then stretched out beside her husband. They lay quietly for a time, sated with food and beauty and savoring the rich gift of time to play and sing and just be together.

Joe reached over and took her hand, twining his fingers through hers. "What are you thinking about?"

She turned her head to look at him, marveling at the beauty of his distinguished features gilded by the sun. "I was thinking about how beautiful this land is. It must mean so much to you to see it after all the stories your father and mother have told you about it. You have a lot of family history here, don't you?"

"Yes, just about all my family history is here, and it goes way, way back. There were Becks in several of the Hapsburg courts. One of my ancestors rode with Otto the Great when he defeated the Magyars in their invasion back in the tenth century. The pope later made Otto the Emperor.

That was, in fact, the beginning of the Holy Roman Empire."

"I can see why it's so much easier for you to identify with it than it is for me." She lay quietly for a moment, watching the sunlight glinting off his blond hair. "Joe?"

"Hmm?"

"You are identifying with it, aren't you? You're beginning to feel like part of Austria."

The short silence was broken by his soft answer. "Yes."

Vicki's stomach tightened and took a slow roll.

"Honey . . ."

"What?" She hoped he didn't ask what she was thinking right now.

"My eyes are closing. How would you feel about lying here on this nice soft, warm grass and taking a nap?"

"Oh, I think I'd be willing to make that sacrifice." She was glad to have the subject changed. It was too lovely a day for serious discussions. "Even though I *was* terribly eager to scale all those higher peaks."

"Well, if you really want—"

"It's all right! Don't move. We'd better save our strength in case of another invasion." As she drifted off, covered by a blanket of warm sun, she had the uncomfortable feeling that the invasion had already occurred—and was successful.

By that evening, when they met Anton in his house for "the cocktail and the dinner," they both felt rested, exercised, and disgustingly healthy.

Anton opened the door to them and surveyed them with approval. "Ah, I think you perhaps take the walk today? You have on your faces the sign of the sun."

"We had a wonderful walk, Uncle Anton." Joe shook his hand enthusiastically. "We took the trail you suggested."

Vicki strolled into the living room, Anton's arm around her shoulder, engulfed in his kindly good humor. She had the feeling they were *still* on the trail suggested by Anton. She hoped it stayed wide enough to accommodate all of them.

They had another delightful dinner, the jovial conversation, held scrupulously to English, revealing stories of Anton's and Rudolph's early childhood years. It was hard for Vicki to picture Joe's father here. Even with his still-strong accent, he seemed thoroughly American.

She heard Anton's tone turn serious, and she listened more closely. "Josef, how are Rudolph and his Maria? His health, it worries me. Always he has the problem, since his sickness. He was so strong, such an athlete, until he has the rheumatic fever. I was only just six. I can remember praying each night to the Virgin, to the saints, 'Please, do not let my brother die.' I wish that he would take from me the money, for a vacation if not for other things. But he is proud, and—what is your word?"

"Stubborn?"

"Yes, yes, that is it. Stubborn."

They all smiled at that. The image of Rudolph straightening his shoulders and setting his chin had to be familiar to all of them.

"Always he was stubborn. But that was a good thing. I think that is why he lived." Anton was gazing off to some distant past, his voice becoming very soft. "Always I am missing Rudolph."

Vicki studied his face, so concerned, so full of love when he spoke of his older brother. He was a very complex man, this uncle of Joe's.

"Victoria, Josef has told me you do the work with the children?"

She stared for a moment, trying to shift gears. Anton was just like Joe; his mind leaped with incredible facility from subject to subject. "Yes. We are lucky enough to have a good special-services department in the school system I work in. Children are having more and more problems these days. There are so many broken homes, and most of the mothers have to work. Lots of the kids spend most of their time outside school with sitters or, worse, alone."

"And you are the . . . executive . . . of this department?"

She laughed. "That's not exactly how I'm listed. I'm the special services director."

"Is that not very good, for one so young?"

"Well, I *have* been lucky. The opportunities for advancement have come along quite swiftly."

Joe jumped in with obvious pride. "Vicki is too modest. You're right, Uncle Anton. It's a very good position for someone as young as she is."

Anton looked thoughtful. "We are having the problem, too, in the business. The women have troubles with the children. I think it would be a good thing to have help for them in our company. Maybe we can talk again, yes? Maybe you could give to me the ideas?"

"I'd be glad to try."

Just then Louisa came into the room, bearing a large plate of delicious-smelling pastries.

"Ah." Anton reached for the serving spatula. "We have the raspberry tarts for dessert. We will put the muscles on you, Victoria, yes?"

"Oh," she moaned, "I'm afraid you mean the pounds. And yes, you certainly will."

She and Joe excused themselves early that night, both sleepy from the long walk and the mixture of fresh air, sunshine, and rich food.

They went upstairs and made love, sweet, close-clinging love that brought back some of Vicki's ease of mind. Only a couple more days before they would leave for Switzerland—she could hardly wait. She and Joe badly needed some time alone. She felt they were rolling, more and more out of control, toward a decision that required more careful consideration than they'd ever given anything before.

The next morning at seven Joe and Vicki joined Anton on his terrace for breakfast. Vicki had rolled out of bed mumbling about the injustice of being aroused that early while she was on vacation, but Joe gently reminded her that the vacation part didn't officially begin until they left for Switzerland.

As they drank a second cup of coffee, Anton said, "Today we have for Joe the work program. I think it is a good idea for him to come to view the business. Victoria, I send our driver to take you to see St. Florian if you wish. Or to the destination you choose."

Vicki gulped and said, "Thank you. That would be very nice." She and Joe exchanged glances. She could see the excitement in his eyes. She wondered if he could see the disappointment in hers.

When they got back upstairs, Vicki said, "I'd like to 'view' the business, too. Do you think he'd consider it rude of me to ask?"

Joe fidgeted, obviously uncomfortable with the question. "I don't imagine he'd think it rude, but I have a feeling he'd prefer it was just the two of us this first time. Will you be unhappy, touring with a stranger? Anton assures me that his driver speaks excellent English and is very amiable."

"No, it's not that I'd be unhappy. It's just...Joe, do you think I could use the extra car—the little Volkswagen? After all, you're going to start trying on a new role. I'd like to do the same. As long as you're not available, I'd rather be completely on my own for the day."

"Honey, are you sure? I mean, you don't speak German at all. What if something happens?"

"What if we were living here and something happened? I can't always have someone around to hold my hand."

"You're right. Would you like me to ask Anton?"

"Please."

Anton had readily agreed, giving her detailed instructions on everything from driving routes to where to park to what to say, in German, to the border guards.

Vicki watched from an upstairs window as the BMW passed through the gate and stopped while Joe jumped out to close and lock it. She looked down at the set of keys in her hand. She must remember to lock the gate when she left.

She delayed her venture into the alien land for a few hours. Pretending all the while that the place was hers, she took a long bath in a tubful of bubbles, then gave herself a leisurely manicure.

After making the bed and putting away the few things that were out of place, she couldn't find much to do. A woman named Sophie came three times a week to clean, a Herr Koerber came twice a week to do general maintenance work, and of course Louisa cooked and shopped and did the dishes.

"And if you lived like this permanently, my dear," she said aloud, "it would leave you with lots and lots and lots of spare time."

Shrugging off the twinge of depression that came with that thought, she got ready for her lone-voyager excursion.

6

BY THE TIME Vicki parked the Volkswagen at a meter in Bad Reichenhall, she was feeling quite proud of herself. Driving here wasn't all that difficult. The traffic signs were clear and Anton's directions explicit. Actually, it was kind of fun being on her own. It gave her a sense of pioneering. She fished around in her change purse, looking for the coin Anton had pointed out as meter-sized. She fit it into the slot and smiled in relief when it slipped in and the meter arm swung to the far side. Success!

She strolled through the charming city, looking at the enticing clothes on display in the shop windows, rapidly calculating their costs in American dollars. This was clearly not a bargain-basement shopping area. She stepped into a produce market, with its fruits and vegetables gaily arranged in large straw baskets, and bought a few apples and oranges and a bundle of asparagus just for the fun of pointing out what she wanted to the cheerful, helpful clerk. Making another excursion into the bakery, where she was tempted by all the yummy aromas, she bought far more than she and Joe and Anton could possibly eat.

Wandering into the meat market, she looked over the fresh cuts of meat, not sure what they all were or how to order. She was intrigued by the yearning she had to cook a full meal herself. She wasn't a wonderful cook, but she did enjoy it when she wasn't wildly busy. Funny, she never would have guessed that being spoiled could grow tiresome. Since she couldn't just point and smile here, she had to forgo buying meat. She marveled at how personal the shopping was, a far cry from American supermarkets.

This town, too, was immaculate, with lovely stretches of manicured lawn and numerous beds of well-tended flowers set among the shops. So different from the streets of Boston! She felt such a twinge of loneliness at the thought of Boston that she shook her head and accelerated her stride, seeking to leave the thought behind.

Eventually she found the structure Anton had told her to be sure to see. It *was* unique. It was a two-story building with slanted walls built for the express purpose of supporting pine boughs, over which there was a steady flow of water.

"The people, they sniff the fumes," Anton had told her. "It is good for the health." She walked all the way around, fascinated by this vacation-spa edifice. Good for the health, was it? Okay, far be it from her to scoff. As she walked, she breathed deeply, giving her lungs the benefit of the good stuff.

Feeling that she had virtuously followed orders and was now full of good vapors, she proceeded to enter one of the shops and spend more on a dress than she ever had in her whole life. That pine-bough cure must do something, she thought as she headed back to the car. She didn't even feel guilty about her extravagance.

She arrived home with barely enough time to wash up and put her purchases away before she heard Anton and Joe come in downstairs.

She raced down to meet them. "Hi, hon." She gave Joe a kiss on his delicious mouth and gave Anton one on the cheek.

"Hi, sweetie." Joe looked tired but exhilarated. "Did you have a good day?"

"Yes, it was fun. How about you?"

"Very, very interesting. That's quite an operation. I have a lot to learn."

Not I *would* have a lot to learn, she noticed.

Anton smiled at her. "It is good you have the fine day. How are you doing on the roads?"

She grinned. "I conquered them with no difficulty. I loved wandering through Bad Reichenhall, and I sniffed the pine-bough fumes like mad. My lungs should be healthy enough to withstand anything. I ate lunch in one of those charming little coffee houses and capped off the day by purchasing an outrageously expensive dress."

"Uh-oh," Joe quipped, "there goes the budget."

"I would like," Anton said, "for the dress to be a gift from me."

"But, Uncle Anton, it already is!" Vicki assured him. "I bought it out of the money you sent."

"No, that is for your travels. I give you the price for the dress. It would please me."

There didn't seem to be much to say to that except thank you.

She and Joe went up to their rooms. His mood was strange. He seemed agreeable but detached, as though all the experiences of the day belonged to him alone, and he was in no hurry to share them. Detachment was practically unknown between them, and it dampened her own spirits considerably.

"Joe?" Her tone was speculative. "Why do you think Anton is in such a hurry to give me things? It makes me nervous."

"He's just trying to please you, honey. You must remember that Anton has no need to worry about money. I should think you'd enjoy being pampered. Heaven knows you've had none of that for at least the last three years."

"I guess." She sank down onto one of the large chairs. "I do believe I'm learning the meaning of an old saying."

"What's that?"

"Too much of a good thing."

Joe came over to sit on the arm of the chair, and he put

his hand on her shoulder. "No one could give you more of a good thing than you deserve."

But who makes the definition, she thought, of "a good thing"?

Joe stood and headed for the bedroom, and Vicki got up and trudged along behind, wondering if he was distracted or if it was her imagination.

"I think I'll get out of this suit and put on some slacks and a sweater." Joe loosened his tie and unbuttoned the stiff collar. "So you liked doing some exploring on your own. Does that mean that you're warming to the idea of the move?"

"Joe, I didn't even think about the move. I was strictly a tourist today. Right now I want to hear all about your day. Was it as exciting as you'd expected?"

Joe took her arm and propelled her to the bed, where they sat side by side as he told her, face aglow, about his experience. "You wouldn't believe it, Vicki. That place is enormous! And there are hundreds of people working for the company—all over the world. I had no conception..." His voice trailed off, and his eyes seemed to film over.

"Joe?" Vicki had a sensation of watching her beloved husband disappearing into a world of his own, to which she could not gain admission. She hoped the sensation wasn't valid.

"What? Oh, sorry. I guess I'm still a bit overwhelmed. Anyway, I met most of the top managers and officers of the company. None of them seemed surprised or upset by my presence. I suspect Anton had prepared them ahead of time."

"Was Gretchen there?"

"Yes, she was. She's a vice-president of marketing. From talking to some of the other men I got the impression that she does a real good job, for a woman."

A sharp stab of shock went through her. "Joe, did you mean that remark?"

"What remark?"

"That Gretchen did a good job *for a woman*. I've never

heard you seriously say anything like that in all the years I've known you."

He got up and went to the bureau, where he fiddled with some of the coins he'd emptied from his pocket. He looked rattled and more than a little annoyed. "Come on, Vicki, I'm just passing along impressions from the others."

"Did she still seem upset about your being here?"

He whirled and faced her. "Dammit! This is the biggest thing that's ever happened to me, and all you can do is carp about how Gretchen feels! She told us herself that even if I fell off the face of the earth she still wouldn't get the executive vice-presidency."

The silence was thunderous. Then Joe broke it by clearing his throat nervously and saying, in a still edgy tone, "I'm sorry. I guess I'm under more strain than I thought. I didn't mean to snap at you." He glanced at the bedside clock. "It's time to go downstairs."

Vicki stood unsteadily, looking across a widening gulf at her husband. "Joe, we need some time to talk. Is there any chance of our having another day by ourselves tomorrow?"

His sheepish look was a prelude to the bad news that followed. "I'm afraid that's not what Anton has in mind. He feels that since we leave so soon I should spend tomorrow at the office, too. He said you could either have another free day, or Gretchen or the driver could take you around."

"Nice. Will they hold my hand, too, and feed me my pabulum?"

"Vicki . . ."

"Sorry. We'd better go down."

The air was heavy with the hastily spoken words, and even heavier with the words left unspoken as they descended the stairs.

As Anton greeted them, he asked, "And is it consented that we go for the dinner at the house of Gretchen and Conrad?"

"Oh, damn," Joe muttered. Then he visibly straightened his spine and said, "I must confess, we started to talk of

other things, and I forgot to mention the invitation to Vicki."
He had blurted it out too fast for Anton to grasp, so Vicki
waited through the suddenly irritating exchange in German.
Joe then turned to her. "Do you mind, Vicki? They'd like
us to come to their house."

She bit back her instinctive response. "No, that's fine."

The house was located on a tree-lined street in a lovely
neighborhood in Bad Reichenhall. Vicki wondered if there
was any significance to the fact that Gretchen and Conrad
lived within the borders of Germany rather than Austria.
She tentatively posed the question to Anton and was informed that Conrad was German, and it was required that
they have their residence in Germany for him to retain ad-
mitting privileges for his patients at the German hospital.

Vicki also wondered, as she stepped out of the car, whether
all the views were spectacular in this part of the world. She
almost longed for a stretch of dull scenery.

They were greeted warmly by Conrad and politely by
Gretchen. When they settled in the comfortable living room
with their wine, Vicki sat next to her, trying to reestablish
the camaraderie they had developed during their day in
Salzburg. "Gretchen," she said, keeping her tone light, "I
hope you and Conrad will be able to visit us in America
sometime soon. It would be fun to show you around Boston."

Gretchen stared at her for a moment, as though weighing
her reply. "Yes, I would like that. We have not had time
to travel. Both Conrad and I have many responsibilities."

Joe jumped in, throwing out a question, as though determined to interrupt the discourse between the two women.
"Conrad, Anton tells me you're considered one of the foremost surgeons in Germany. Do you operate in just one
hospital, or are you affiliated with several, as some American doctors are?"

This touched off a long discussion on the practice of
medicine in Germany, which took up most of the cocktail
hour. The conversation during dinner was held to safe sub-

jects: art, theater, the influence of Mozart on the musical history of Salzburg.

While they were lingering over coffee, Anton said, "Victoria has the fine position of work. She helps children to solve their problems."

"Is that right?" Conrad seemed immediately interested. "What do you do, Vicki?"

"I'm a psychiatric social worker. I work for the public school system in Cambridge. My department handles the special needs of children under twelve. I counsel some youngsters individually, and the rest of my time is spent in administrative work. It's a fulfilling job. I hope to complete my doctorate one day." She smiled at Joe. "But not for a while. We've had enough book-learning for a year or so at least."

Anton leaned forward, that intense look on his face. "Gretchen, you have concern for the mothers who work in our factory. They are having problems with the care for their children. Victoria would be of help in this."

Gretchen looked confused and distraught, and Vicki instinctively knew what was wrong. Anton was not only pushing Joe down her corporate throat, but was now including Vicki in the package.

Suddenly tired of what seemed an advanced case of insensitivity in Anton, Vicki pushed her chair back and said, "I hate to be rude, but I have to admit that I'm very tired. Perhaps the excitement of braving your highways on my own took more of a toll than I realized. Gretchen, if my work is of interest to you, that's a good excuse for you to visit Boston. I'd be delighted to show you our facilities and also explain in detail an experimental program I'm setting up for one of our large local companies. They want to provide day care and counseling services within the structure of the corporation. It'll be in full operation by mid-October. That would be a lovely time to come, since you could also see the autumn foliage."

Gretchen stared at her, then blurted, "But you will not be in Boston by October."

There was a deadly silence in the room. Vicki broke it
by standing and announcing, "I expect to be in Boston in
October. There's no way I could turn over my responsibilities that quickly in any case. And I don't want my decisions
on anything to be taken for granted."

Anton stood quickly. "It is late, and we are all tired. Let
us go home now. Thank you, Gretchen"—he kissed her
cheek—"for the most excellent dinner." He took a few
steps, then stopped. "Oh. It is possible that Victoria needs
you for the tour tomorrow."

Vicki took one look at the other woman's face and stated
bluntly, "No. There's no need for Gretchen to interrupt her
work, which I'm sure is very important, just to take me
around. I'm quite capable of maneuvering on my own. Besides, I think I'll just take a long walk and start reading a
novel I brought with me. Gretchen has been imposed on
enough."

When she said good night, Gretchen gave her a warm
smile and a kiss on the cheek.

Unfortunately, the mood in the car on the ride back didn't
seem as convivial. Even Anton was silent, and Joe seemed
almost hostile.

By the time Joe and Vicki were in their room preparing
for bed, she was so tired she simply wanted to collapse
without speaking another word. But Joe wasn't about to
leave it alone.

"Vicki, don't you think that was spreading it on a little
thick? Nobody's trying to make your decisions for you, and
it seems pretty ungrateful, after everything Anton's done
for us, to start giving him little jabs about how he deals
with his own daughter. That's his business."

She whirled on him, all reserve gone, the frustration of
the situation taking control. "Damn it all, that's just not
true! The pressures may be subtle, but they're there. And
I'm *not* trying to tell Anton how to deal with Gretchen, but
I'm also not willing to buy into that unfair charade. I don't
know why she doesn't scream and yell and stamp her feet
when he treats her like a readily available tour guide. I'll

bet he wouldn't send Herr Hollweg or Herr Berchtold out to drive me around!" To her vexation, she felt the tears start to run down her cheeks. "I don't know what you want anymore, Joe. You tell me how much you love me just the way I am; then you get mad at me for not being different!"

Joe crossed to her quickly, pulling her close and making soothing sounds. "Honey, don't cry. You're absolutely right, and I'm being totally unfair."

"Darn it," she sniffed, "I hate to cry when we're fighting. It makes me feel so . . . female!"

"Vicki, my darling, you *are* female. And crying gives you an advantage. I can't stand to see you cry."

"I don't know why not. It's no big deal. People cry all the time." She held on to him tightly. "Oh, Joe, I've felt so lonely since you got back this evening—as if you were drawing away from me!"

"Never. Not ever. No matter what, it's the two of us together against the world." He drew her over close enough to the chest of drawers to reach the box of tissues on top. He took one out and dabbed at her wet cheeks. "Vicki, I really am sorry, but we mustn't let any of this come between us. Whatever we do, we have to do it together."

She studied his handsome face, the forehead wrinkled in uncharacteristic worry lines. "Oh, Joe, we do have to, don't we! I couldn't possibly live without you. I'd be lonely for the rest of my life. Honey, let's go to bed and cuddle. Just wrap our arms around each other and hold on for dear life."

"That's just what you are, Vicki. You're everything that's dear to me in life." He knew that was true, but he didn't know how it would magically erase their problems.

His mind continued its troubled roll as they undressed, meticulously hanging up their clothes, folding garments and placing them neatly in drawers, Vicki even taking time to rinse out her lingerie. Why were they constrained by this unfamiliar, unwelcome formality?

Suddenly, for one of the few times in his life, Joe felt fear. Everything he wanted in the world was almost in the palm of his hand. Would it slip away? His mind-screen was

suddenly filled with an unwanted image of Gretchen, her
empty hands turned up helplessly on a tabletop. Damn. Why
was there nothing on the face of the earth that was simple?

His eyes moved back to his wife. Even this monumental,
encompassing, heretofore simply perfect relationship was
developing cracks. Nooks and crannies—an American
expression his mother had adopted with glee. "They are
everywhere, Josef," she would solemnly assure him, "the
nooks and crannies. Even in the union of two people with
much love."

When they were undressed and had clean teeth and faces,
they crawled into bed and reached almost timidly for each
other. Whatever happened to throwing their clothes any
which way and diving for the bed, scarcely taking time to
pull down the covers?

Joe drew Vicki's warm, nude body to his, wrapping his
arms around her gently, then tighter and tighter as the fear
increased. Vicki's cheeks were still damp. Oh, God, that
made him almost sick. He brushed his hand over her hair,
over and over in a consoling gesture, then stopped abruptly
as he remembered Vicki didn't like that. She had laughingly
told him it made her feel like his dog.

Laughingly. What a keynote of their marriage. So much
in their years together had been done laughingly. Full of
joy. He mustn't, mustn't destroy that.

But what was he to do with this burning hunger in him?
Was it wealth he lusted for? He honestly didn't think so.
Certainly he bowed to its appeal but, being as honest with
himself as he could be, it wasn't the most compelling at-
traction. The main thing he wanted from money was freedom from worry about it. After all the years of scraping
and juggling bills and doing without, that would sure as hell
be nice.

As he lay there, aware of the indescribable pleasure of
holding Vicki, of the warmth of her skin against his, of the
solace that seeped like balm from her pores to his, he tried
to pinpoint the pole of the magnet that drew him to this job.
He knew that most men would say, "Are you nuts? Who
wouldn't be drawn? Grab it!" But Joe was far too analytical

to let it go at that. There was too much at stake. He was asking Vicki to abandon her home and follow him to a new country, and although women had been following their men to new places for ages past, things were different now. Women were different now. They wanted to know *why* first, and Joe couldn't quarrel with that. He liked Vicki's independence. He had no wish to squelch it.

So, Mr. Beck, he asked himself, why do you want to stay in Austria? No ready, easy answer leaped to mind. Joe sifted through the myriad sensations that had engulfed him since their arrival. He liked Anton, genuinely liked him. The man was good and kind and concerned about people. It was also clear, after just one day of watching him in his work environment, that he was an astute, infinitely capable businessman, respected and well liked by his employees.

In short, Anton was extraordinary. And Anton had offered *him* the highest job available in his company. So Anton must consider him to be of like caliber. And what man does not want to be regarded as extraordinary? So, number one: ego. But the compliment had been given. He could leave Austria tomorrow and take the ego boost with him. That still wasn't the core of his reason for wanting to stay here and take the job. The core was something that had been part and parcel of his nature for as long as he could remember, and it all came back to the hunger. A driving, demanding hunger for achievement.

Joe ran his hand over Vicki's smooth skin. She was asleep. So precious. She was so precious. His hand slid down her back and over the rise of her tightly rounded rear. Despite his tiredness and his distraction, he could feel the beginnings of arousal. But he wouldn't bother her; she'd been so distressed by the evening.

Vicki. How he loved her! She completed him, made him whole, filled a void he hadn't known existed until he fell in love with her. Love. Even more difficult to define than ambition. But they were both there—strong, demanding, inescapable. How in God's name was all this going to work out?

He knew there was yet another problem to be dealt with.

Regardless of how he might try to sidestep any responsibility, he was not totally unsympathetic to Gretchen's plight.
He just didn't know what to do about it. Among other things.

Just then Vicki stirred in his arms. "Joe?"

"What?"

"You still awake?"

"Uh-huh."

"How come?"

"I didn't want to go to sleep yet. I was afraid if I went
to sleep you'd slip away and leave me."

"I'll never leave you."

"Promise?"

"Promise."

Promises, promises. So easy to give and so hard to keep.
"Vicki?"

"Hmm?"

"I love you."

"I love you, too." She snuggled closer, then said, "Joe . . ."

"What?"

"Will you make love to me? No flashing lights; just come
into me so we can be as close as possible."

He moved on top of her and slid into her, not moving
for the moment, just staying closer than close.

"That's better," she murmured. "That feels so good, so
safe."

"Yes." There seemed nothing to add. "Yes." Slowly at
first, then with growing urgency, he moved within her and
reached his climax. Sweet, sweet completion.

"Don't go away." Her voice was fuzzy with impending
sleep.

"I won't." He stayed there, tucked inside, life to life.
Just as he drifted off to sleep he realized that Vicki's cheeks
were still damp. But then, so were his.

The morning light flooded the apartment, filling it with
hope and the optimism born of a new day. Joe straightened
his tie and called in to Vicki, who was still in the bathroom.
"Hey, hon. What are you going to do today?"

She came out, dressed in teal blue shorts, a white shirt, and white sneakers. Her eyes were a tiny bit puffy, but she still looked beautiful. "I am going to pack a lunch and walk. It's sheer madness to be in a place like this and not take complete advantage of the beauty of the outdoors. I'll give a sympathetic thought or two to you, poor thing, cooped up within the bricks and mortar of enterprise."

Joe grinned at her, grateful for her lightened mood, grateful to her for presenting it to him—her morning gift. "That's a great idea. Ask Anton at breakfast; he knows all the good trails."

"I will. I'll also ask him how far he's willing to go on this let's-spoil-Vicki route. As long as he's being so cavalier with his money, I might go back to Bad Reichenhall and buy out the town."

"Uh-oh. That might destroy even Anton's budget!" They were able to tease lightheartedly again. They were back on *laughingly*. What a pleasure. "Vicki . . ."

She stopped brushing her hair and turned away from the mirror, her attention caught by his serious tone. "Yes?"

"Can we make a pact? Let's get through the day and try not to worry about the future. We leave tomorrow for Switzerland, and I, for one, am more than ready to unwind and put all the problems and decisions on ice for a few days. Do you think we could? Let's see . . . We'll be gone for a week. Shall we agree—no serious discussions until next Thursday afternoon?"

Vicki's face lit up. She stepped forward and thrust out her hand. "My good man, you have a deal." They shook hands vigorously.

Vicki spent the whole morning walking through the hills, thoroughly refreshed by communing with nature, determinedly adhering to the morning agreement, and forcibly expelling problems from her mind. It was a good exercise, and it worked. Before long she found herself simply enjoying the trees and the mountains and the birds and the fresh air.

*   *   *

She and Joe made love again that night, managing to recapture some of the old abandon. The feeling of freedom with which they had started this journey was making a slow comeback. They were to have seven whole days alone— and in Switzerland! Surely that magic land they'd both fantasized about would repair any small fissures in their relationship.

Vicki fell asleep with visions of Swiss Alps floating in her head. They were bound to be different from Austrian and German Alps, weren't they?

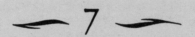

7

WHEN JOE AND Vicki were shown to their room at the Hôtel de la Paix in Geneva, they shot each other a raised-eyebrows here-we-go-again look. The room was enormous, with a balcony that overlooked the Rhône River. To their left, where the river widened and joined Lake Geneva, was the famous Jet d'Eau, the world's tallest fountain, spouting up a plume of white water from the clear blue surface.

Joe tipped the bellhop and joined Vicki on the balcony, draping a possessive arm around her shoulder. "Do you realize that we are actually, for the first time in the three years of our marriage, alone together with no responsibilities but to have a good time for seven whole days?"

"No. As yet my psyche is still in high gear. So far this 'vacation' has been exhausting." She wrapped her arms around his waist and looked up at him pleadingly. "Joe, could we have our dinner sent up? It's so lovely right here on the balcony, and it's fun to watch the people strolling by below us on the street and look at the peaceful river right over there across the street. I'd like to just sit and not think about anything. In fact, if you're up to it, I'd appreciate it if you'd order the dinner. And don't ask me what I want, because that would involve a decision."

He laughed and kissed her cheek. "Okay, done. I will take full responsibility for the rest of the day and night. Do I get the feeling that you're calling for complete rest—not even a little wild sex mixed in?"

"You've got it. Not even a little tame sex mixed in. I long to be cared for—fed, pampered, and indulged—but by *you* this time."

The message was clear.

"Most of all I want my mind to lie fallow, even to fall on its side in a dead faint for at least twenty-four hours."

"I can tell you're going to be inspiring company. Maybe I'd better start that book I brought along. Better still, maybe I should eat with you, tuck you into bed, then go case the strip show at the Pussy Cat Saloon to make sure it's fit viewing for my sheltered, midwestern, morality-clad wife."

"Oh, no you don't. *I'm* the one who wanted to go in the first place! I've never been to a real live strip show, and I've been told that the Pussy Cat's is one of the best. And don't try to weasel out of it. You promised you'd take me. My midwestern morality will survive. I promise to be fully recovered from my temporary weariness by the morrow."

"The Morrow. Isn't that four days after Easter?"

"Joe . . ."

"Okay, okay. I'll be good. And as soon as you lift the no-sex ban, I'll try to be fantastic." Before she could land the swat she aimed in his direction, he jumped back and, chuckling smugly at his own repartee, began the task of unpacking his suitcase.

Vicki put her clothes away, surprised by the weight of weariness that lay on her. Funny, once again she felt wiped out while Joe was, as her mother would put it, full of beans.

The last few years of endless work had taken their toll, but any negative feelings had been fleeting. The close, loving marvel of her relationship with Joe had more than made up for the tiredness then. So why this depressed exhaustion now, of all times? Right now she wanted, more than anything, to *feel* as if she was on vacation. Oh, well, probably all she needed was a good night's sleep.

She carried her toiletry bag into the bathroom. "Ye gods!"

Joe rushed in. "What's the matter?"

Vicki turned to him, her head tilted quizzically, her hands on her hips. "Is this all part of your bathroom-fetish plot? Never in my entire life would I have dreamed there were so many marble wonders in the world. People could *live* in these bathrooms...be born, make babies, and expire in these bathrooms! It seems indecently lush somehow."

"Honey?"

"What?"

"I think you're developing a fixation on bathrooms."

"You think *I*—" Her fatigue disappeared like magic as she lit into her husband, pummeling him with ineffective blows and finally collapsing in helpless laughter on, of course, the carpeted bathroom floor.

"Now see?" Joe had her pinned, his body fully on top of hers. "It's just as I suspected. All this harping was merely a ruse to lure me to the bathroom floor. You didn't want to miss even one opportunity, did you, you little devil you. All along you've had this wild, uncontrollable desire to try them all—all the elegant bathrooms across Europe. How am I going to control your mad, rampant fixation when we go out to dinner, or—dear God, the thought is frightening—if you visit the ladies' room at the Pussy Cat Saloon?"

"Joe!" Vicki's struggles accomplished nothing. She was giggling too hard to fight effectively.

"I had best be prepared"—he kissed her neck, then buried his lips in the ticklish spot in the hollow at the base of her throat—"for all types of drastic measures. I shall have to carry a small bag full of women's clothes and spot a hiding place where I can conceal myself long enough to change. Then I can answer your desperate call at any time, any place." He ran his hand up the inside of her thigh and slipped his warm fingers under the easily bypassed panties.

"Joe, let me up! This is not on the program!"

"Don't fight it. I've read that sexual obsessions, unless harmful, should be indulged."

The intruding fingers had intruded still farther, causing her to gasp and also causing her to stop struggling quite so hard.

"There, you see? You're giving in to your crazy compulsion. That's good."

The fingers were moving in her, sending tingling torrents from inside out, invading all the surrounding territory.

"Go with it. Don't fight it. That's my girl. Lush, thick bathroom carpeting is perfect for writhing."

"That does it! Now let me up! I really do not want to make love on the bathroom floor—this or any other!"

The fingers slowly withdrew, giving a teasing tickle on the way. Joe slipped down and planted a ceremonious kiss on each of her knees. "All right. If you're determined to fight it. But there. At least the knees have been kissed. If a fit of bathroom fetish is cut off before the knees have been kissed, it's dangerous to the sanity."

"The only danger to my sanity is you!"

About the time they had finished putting all their clothes away and used the bathroom for the more seemly purpose of bathing, the waiter appeared at the door with a bottle of Dom Perignon, compliments of Anton, and a platter of assorted canapés, which included pâté and caviar and crackers so thin and crisp that Vicki and Joe deliberated on whether to eat them or post them with a "fragile" sign. The vote to eat them carried.

While Vicki sat, enthralled by the light shimmering on the shooting spire of the Jet d'Eau, Joe went to the phone to order sole Grand Vefour for Vicki and duck with three-pepper sauce for himself.

They ate on the balcony, the air warm and clean around them, the quiet murmur of conversation between the passersby on the street below creating a convivial background for their private meal.

Vicki leaned back and, with a sigh, carefully set her cup back in its saucer. "Joe?"

"What, my love?"

"Let's push this little table outside the door and go to bed and get a nice, long night's sleep. And when we wake up in the morning, I promise to be totally, completely *on vacation*. Okay?"

"Sounds good to me."

Within twenty minutes they were in bed. Joe fell asleep almost immediately, but Vicki, who needed to, didn't. Her unruly mind wound around and around, covering over-tracked, off-limits territory again and again before she finally dropped into a deep slumber.

The next morning, however, true to her word, she woke up feeling like a vacationer. She hummed as she dressed in a pale green summer wool skirt and a beige short-sleeved blouse with tiny green pinstripes. Joe, his everyday, part-and-parcel elegance intact, wore his "uniform"—tan slacks, white dress shirt open at the neck, and navy blue blazer.

He held Vicki's beige cotton jacket as she slipped her arms in. "Gosh, you're pretty," he said.

She made a deliberately flirtatious gesture out of pushing her curly brown hair outside her collar and blinked her long lashes at him. "Why, thank you, kind sir." They stood side by side, assessing their appearance in the wide mirror over the bureau.

"All in all, I must admit, we're a stunning couple," she pronounced.

"Stunning, or stunned?"

"Both," she agreed. She picked up her purse. "Okay, where are we going? Do we have any plans?" She opened her green eyes to full width, giving him a deliberate take-care-of-me look.

"We are going to buy you a gen-u-wine Swiss watch, like it tells ya you should otta do in all the travel ads."

"Sure we are. And where is the gen-u-wine loot going to come from?"

"From my own little piggy bank. I've been squirreling away semi-vast sums for the last year to buy you a proper thanks-for-the-help present. Since you have griped, almost without cease, I might add, about your cheap, tinny watch, that seemed most appropriate. And"—he held up a hand to stop her amazed reaction—"since I know that half the fun is in the selection, I figured we'd do that together."

"Oh, Joe!" Vicki threw her arms around him and gave him a resounding kiss. She made no protest since, number one, she knew it would do no good, and number two, she wanted the watch.

That night, dressed up in her new smoky-topaz silk Bad Reichenhall dress and wearing her new Swiss watch, Vicki walked proudly through the hotel lobby with her arm linked through her husband's, experiencing the pleasurable taste of affluence. She felt beautiful, and she enjoyed the admiring glances she was getting from the well-heeled men she passed.

"You know," she quipped, "I'm beginning to suspect that being poor isn't all it's cracked up to be."

"Oh, yeah? Just wait until you've put up with wealth for a while. Then you'll sing a different tune!"

They walked down the street to the Richemonde for cocktails, then back up along the river for dinner at the Café du Rhône. They both wanted to see it all, and they were staying in Geneva for only two days. They tarried over their delicious meal, chatting in an effortless flow the way they always had before this wonderful-terrible new dimension had been added to their lives. When they finally stepped out in front to get a taxi, it was quite late and there were no cabs in sight.

Joe was exasperated. "Now what are we going to do? We only have this one night here in Geneva, and I *have* to get you to that strip show. If we don't get there, what will I tell my friends? The only reason my wife wanted to come to Switzerland was to see a risqué show, and I failed in my duty to provide transportation?"

"Joe, don't you dare tell your buddies that that was the reason I wanted to come. I know that group; I'd never hear the last of it!"

"Listen, you're already famous at Harvard. You're the only woman any of the students, professors, or administrative personnel had ever heard of who would travel all this way to see naked women. It raised certain questions, which I did my best to lay to rest."

"Joe, why do I get the awful feeling that I shouldn't just laugh that off? I'll bet you *did* tell everyone I wanted to go!"

"You're darned right. I wouldn't miss such an opportunity. But now we must *get* you there!"

He glanced down the street and spotted a woman who, with the assistance of the cab driver, was juggling boxes at the back of a taxi. "Let's go!" He grabbed Vicki's hand and headed for the cab.

"How do you know she isn't getting in instead of out?"

"I don't. But if we stand here we'll miss it in either case."

When they reached their destination, they saw, with visible disappointment, that the boxes were being wedged *into* the trunk. The woman clucked at them sympathetically. "Oh, you vanted zee taxi? Zo zorry. Eet ees necessaree zat I go with ze wind!"

Vicki leaned close to Joe and whispered in his ear, "She sounds like you do when you're kidding!"

Joe gave her a nudge, then turned his most persuasive smile—which was very persuasive indeed—on the woman. "You're right. We thought maybe you were arriving instead of leaving. My wife and I are here on our honeymoon"—another nudge to Vicki to keep her quiet—"and we have only two days in Geneva. We were hoping to go to the Pussy Cat Saloon. Some of our friends told us it was wonderful fun. I don't suppose you're heading in that direction?"

Vicki couldn't believe his audacity. Their honeymoon indeed!

"Zee honeymoon!" The woman grabbed the sleeve of the taxi driver, who had come out of the door of the small hotel doing a rather impressive balancing act with a stack of her boxes.

"Please!" he protested. "I'm about to drop these as it is!" He continued to wedge the boxes into the trunk on top of those already there.

"Iss fate, iss fate!" The exotic woman gave each of them an exuberant hug. "You go to zee Poosy Cat. *I* go to zee Poosy Cat. Zo . . . you ride weeth me! Now! Iss fate, no?"

Joe's smile widened. "It is fate indeed. You came to our rescue! Can I help with the boxes?"

With an incredible number of boxes stashed in the trunk and the front seat, and the three of them in the rear, they took off for the strip show. Joe, acting as self-appointed master of ceremonies, said, "I'm Josef Beck, and this is my wife, Vicki."

"How zweet. How zweet iss younk luff! Me, I am Madame Vooska. I am Hoongarian! I am not havink the luff in my life joost now, but I am havink mooch of it in my time!" This sent Madame Vooska off into peals of laughter.

Vicki was spellbound. It was hard to imagine the woman as the object of a lover's affection. She appeared to be around sixty, with a swarthy complexion and gray-streaked black hair that stuck out in tendrils through a heavy, bright red hair net. Despite the warm night air, she wore a black coat buttoned to the neck, with a red scarf thrown about her throat. She looked exotic, strange, and as far as Vicki was concerned, altogether wonderful.

"Did you say you were actually going to the Pussy Cat or just near it?" She tried to keep her tone conversational. No need to telegraph her incredulity over the idea of the visitor from Hungary attending what was reputed to be a rather explicit strip show.

This sent the colorful woman into another explosion of mirth. One thing about Madame Vooska, she sure seemed to enjoy life. "I go, I go!" she shrieked through her hilarity. "Zee girls, zay vait for zee Madame. Vithout me iss not zo goot, zee show!"

"I beg your pardon?"

The cab had stopped in front of the nightclub, and any further questions were postponed while boxes were unloaded and put on the sidewalk. While Joe paid the fare, Madame Vooska dashed inside and reappeared followed by two burly young men. They scooped up the boxes as Madame Vooska issued a steady stream of largely unintelligible orders, then disappeared inside.

"See?" Joe whispered. "I told you I'd get you here."

"Sure," Vicki whispered back, watching the strange proceedings warily. "But what did you get us into?"

The woman motioned them to join her at the door, where she announced, presumably to the world, "Thees are my goot frenns. Iss Josef and Veeki. Zay vill sit at my table!" With that she vanished through a side door.

Completely confused, Joe and Vicki followed the maître d' through the packed tables to a booth that was directly beside the step-up stage. It was the only empty table in the place. When they were seated and had ordered a drink, Vicki said, "Joe, who on earth do you suppose—"

"I haven't the foggiest."

The lights dimmed, and the show started. The advertising was truthful; it was quite a show, done with taste and a touch of class, and boasting a bevy of gorgeous girls. Vicki was delighted. "A real, live strip show!" she crowed. "It makes me feel so deliciously decadent."

"Uh-oh," Joe moaned. "Bye-bye to our little country girl; hello to the hardened woman of the world."

"Isn't that what you're trying to accomplish?" When she saw Joe's look, she was sorry she'd said it. It hadn't come out funny.

About half an hour into the show, Madame Vooska slid into the booth. "Iss vonderful, no? Zee girls, zay are be-ootiful?"

"They certainly are." Joe looked glassy-eyed.

"Stop breathing so hard," Vicki lectured. "This is supposed to be *my* big experience!"

One of the numbers had just finished, and to their amazement, instead of making an exit as the others had, the stripper made a signal to a shadowy person in the wings, who handed her a robe. The girl then proceeded to come to their table and sit down, right next to Joe. Completely ignoring both of them, the girl and Madame Vooska launched into a rapid dialogue, complete with hand gestures that were, to say the least, interesting.

During the next thirty or forty minutes, the routine was repeated with every performer, and there were often three or four of the girls jammed into their booth at once. Joe was openly envied by every male in the house. When the lights went up for intermission, the last remaining showgirl gasped, "Oh! I've got to change my costume for the next act!" and dashed off.

"What costume?" Vicki asked incredulously.

"Ah, zat girl, she has zee beoooty costume. *I* make zee costume!"

The light began to dawn.

"Is that what this is all about?" Joe leaned toward her, his face bright with curiosity. "You make the costumes?"

"Yes, yes! I am zee best in zee world!"

"No wonder those boxes were so light," he mumbled.

"Ah, you zee, eet ees zee secret! Zee clothes must come off—zip! Like zat!"

"I can't quarrel with that," Joe agreed. "They certainly come off 'zip, like that!' How do you decide what kind of costume to make for whom?"

"Eet depend on zee sooccess of zee girl. Zee more zee sooccess, zee longer zee act, zee more she pay, zee more vast zee costume! You see?"

It was almost perfectly clear. For the rest of the evening, Joe and Vicki watched with increased interest the "vastness" of the costume and the time it took the girl to disrobe. Some of the numbers did involve elaborate outfits, and the disrobing was a longer, more teasing affair. These girls were clearly the more successful. They were also the more beautiful and the ones who spent longer stretches of time at the table making larger and more graphic hand gestures. Vicki noticed they were also the ones who got the most attention from her husband.

By the beginning of the late show, which was, they were

informed, a repeat of what had already been performed, Joe and Vicki were more than ready to call it a night. They bid a fond, hugging adieu to their Hungarian hostess and stepped outside, where they both collapsed against the wall, weak with laughter.

"I never," Vicki gasped between giggles, "expected that one of the most enjoyable learning experiences I would ever have would concern the dressing—and undressing—of strippers!"

Joe was rubbing his eyes. "My eyes are all dried out. I haven't blinked for three hours!"

"Oh, Joe, what a marvelous first night of our official vacation! Wasn't that fun? And wasn't Madame Vooska marvelous?"

"She was marvelous, delightful, and thoroughly enchanting. She was the hit of the evening." To Vicki's skeptical look he countered, "Would I lie?" His starched eyes made the innocent expression difficult.

"I take all my objections back," Vicki giggled. "You may tell everyone at home that tonight was well worth the whole trip!"

Joe kissed her, right there in front of the Pussy Cat billboards. "I'm glad. I'm glad it was better than you'd expected." The rest of that statement—*It's the only part of the trip that has been*—didn't need to be spoken.

This time they had no trouble hailing a cab, and before long they were in bed holding each other tight, still chuckling about their newfound friend.

"Can't you just see them, Joe, those fifteen women she employs? They're probably middle-aged and rather staid, all sewing away in some garret, turning out wispy creations that come off 'zip! like that!'"

"Speaking of stripping, what's with this obstacle between us?"

"Obstacle? That's my brand-new, bought-in-Austria, sexy-as-all-hell nightgown!"

"Would you be terribly offended if I told you I think you're sexier in the nude?"

"I'll have to give that some thought. It's rather sad to realize that a pure silk, slinky nightgown has no effect on you."

"Not true. It fills me with an overwhelming compulsion to remove it."

"Thank heaven. I was beginning to fear it was a complete flop."

With Vicki's active cooperation, the nightie was soon gracing the carpet next to the bed.

"Okay, 'fess up. Is it me you're thinking of right now? Is it *my* body you're running your hands over, or am I only a poor stand-in for one of Madame Vooska's gorgeous customers?"

"You know I only have eyes for you, Sonia...uh... Letitia..."

"Sonia, eh? You know of course that she was the cute blonde who wanted to wear hot pink feathers."

"Hot pink...one of my favorite colors. Did you know that you have body parts that turn hot pink when—"

"Joe, do that again...mmmm, yes, that's wonderful. Just keep it up. I'll tell you when to stop."

"I'm doing my best to keep it up. You could help a little, you know."

"Gladly. What would you like me to do? Joe, that's an evil laugh. This is a high-class bed we're making love in. I think whipped cream would be frowned on by the management."

"How do you think they'd feel about nude bodies running through the halls?"

"Your Uncle Anton the empire builder would be less than amused if his genius nephew was tossed out of the Hôtel de la Paix. Particularly if his new accommodation was the local jail."

"My Uncle Anton has no word in this. He's way off in Austria."

"Tell that to the cashier."

"Listen, my pretty pigeon, these are *my* hot hands on your warm, delectable flesh. Please do not interject names of other men into our bed-warming."

"So? Who plopped Sonia and Letitia right down on the sheets? Oooh, keep on doing that and I'll forgive you your indiscretion."

"How about if I do this? You sort of like that, don't you?"

"I do like that . . . oh, Joe . . ."

"Vicki, Vicki, you are so delicious. Hold me, honey . . . That's right, just like that . . . Vicki . . ."

"Joe . . . Joe . . . Joe . . . please, now, Joe, now!"

They both slept very well.

After a delightful breakfast on the balcony, Joe went downstairs to check out while Vicki called to have their rented car delivered. The desk clerk gave Joe a copy of the bill, which was staggering, but informed him that all costs had been covered. Joe struggled between relief and a strange discomfort over being "cared for." Was this what working for Anton would feel like—this Big Brother is watching you sensation? Or in this case, Big Uncle?

A man in a black cap approached him. "Mr. Beck?"

"Yes."

"Your car is outside, sir. It's a Jaguar. I hope that is satisfactory."

"The car is here already? My wife was just calling when I came down."

"The bell captain notified us as soon as you let him know you were checking out. We like to give good service, sir."

"That's kind of you. I'm impressed. Uh, just as a matter of curiosity, do you know who made the car reservation?"

The man glanced at the sheet of paper he was holding. "A Mr. Hollweg, from Linz." He looked at Joe, a worried line across his forehead. "If you don't like the car, we'd be glad to arrange for another, sir."

"Oh, no, that won't be necessary. I think we can manage all right with a Jaguar. It's a *new* Jaguar, I assume."

"Oh, yes, sir, of course."

"I'll go up to tell my wife we're ready. Shall I take the keys now?"

"No, sir, I'll wait until you come back. You may have some questions about the car."

"Fine." Joe went to the elevator and pushed the button for their floor. A new Jag—Anton was really laying it on. Well, he wasn't about to look a gift Jaguar in the mouth— or engine, as the case may be. Wait until Vicki got a load of this.

By the time they left the city and headed toward Montreux, Joe was really getting the feel of the car. "Vicki, I want to tell you, this is one nice machine. I could get used to this."

"I have a feeling that's the idea."

"To get us used to all this?"

"Right."

"Let's be big about it and give it a shot. We can always choose poverty later, after we've had a chance to fully sample the alternative."

"Joe?"

"What?"

"Oh, never mind. We'll talk about it later. It's such a gorgeous day and such a gorgeous view. We should just enjoy it." She wished she could shake the cloying sensation of being subtly seduced by long-distance. The Jaguar was spectacular. Why on earth did she wish it were a Ford? Well, they'd talk about it later, like Thursday.

The next two days were sheer, unadulterated pleasure for both of them. They found, much to their delight, that the reservations they had were in a small, intimate country hotel outside of Montreux. Their room was large and sunny and filled with bouquets of fresh flowers. It was a corner room with balconies on two sides, one overlooking the lake in the distance and the other providing a sweeping vista of a meadow backed by a mountain. Joe called Anton to tell him how pleased they were. He was delighted to hear from them.

On the second day of their stay they got a lunch packed by the charming cook-proprietress and drove farther into the hills for a hike and a picnic. As they were laying out the checked cloth and unwrapping the cheese and bread and salami, Vicki stopped. "Joe, listen to that! Why in the world would someone have a cuckoo clock way out here?"

"Honey, that's not a clock. That's a real cuckoo bird."

"You're joshing me."

"Not at all. Vicki, didn't you know they were real birds?"

She stared down at the picnic repast for a moment, then sheepishly met Joe's eyes. They burst out laughing. "My, my," she marveled, "the things I'm learning on this trip! By the time I get home, I'll be a walking encyclopedia of useless information!" When I get home. *When.*

During the night Joe started to sneeze. He sneezed and sneezed, keeping both of them awake until the wee hours. By morning his nose was red and his eyes running.

"Joe, what rotten luck, you're getting a cold."

"I am *not* getting a cold. It's a touch of hay fever, that's all."

"You don't get hay fever."

"Oh, yeah? Well, what do you call this, then?"

"A cold."

"Damn it all to hell, it isn't a cold! Why do you have to keep insisting I have a cold? What makes you so blinking sure it's a cold?"

"Because when you get a head cold, you also get a sinus headache, which makes you short-tempered."

"Who the hell says I'm short-tempered? I'm calm as a cucumber!"

"Who the hell says a cucumber is calm?"

Joe did his best to ignore the rapidly worsening symptoms, but by the following morning he was miserable. He woke up, after a fitful, on-and-off sleep, and said, "Vicki, I think I have a cold."

"Really?" She opened her mouth to give him the jab he deserved for his foul temper of the previous day, but one look at his puffy eyes and the lines of pain around them shut her up. "Oh, Joe, you poor thing. The headache has really got you, hasn't it?"

"It's awful. This bloody, rotten sinus!"

"We're going to have to find a doctor."

"I don't know if I can get out of bed to see a doctor. I'm too sick."

"Madame Clouet must know someone. I'll go down and ask."

"What time do we have to check out?"

"Honey, you're too sick to travel. I'll see if we can stay here for another day or two."

"And miss Zermatt? Not on your life! I'll be fine."

"Joe . . ." She closed her mouth once again. She knew how fruitless it was to try to reason with him in this condition. Sinus headaches were the only thing she knew to bring out the Mr. Hyde side of Joe.

Two hours later they were sitting in a room in the rear of a house that served as the office for Dr. André Vionne. Dr. Vionne spoke not one word of any language but French, and Vicki and Joe were both hopeless in French.

"Le nose!" Joe shouted. As the communication became more difficult, the speech became slower and louder. "Le head, she ache." His hands flailed around his eyes. "See? Drip, drip."

"Joe, he's not retarded; he just doesn't speak English."

"Well, why the hell doesn't he? Everyone should speak English!" He returned to the hand gestures. "Pound, pound! How can this guy live in Switzerland and not at least speak German?"

"Ah!" The doctor was beginning to catch on to the sign language. He imitated Joe, banging his fingers against his head. *"Oui?"*

"That's it! And uh . . ." Joe's fingers rippled down from his nose.

"Ah!" Once again, the diagnosis was made.

Vicki was having an awful time. The laughter kept bubbling up inside, threatening to erupt at any second. This consultation was the closest thing to a Laurel and Hardy routine she'd seen in years. "By George, I think he's got it!" she whispered.

The explanation of treatment was even funnier. The doctor wrote out five prescriptions, and with each there came a visual demonstration. The first was to be put in the mouth—he popped an imaginary pill into his mouth and drank it down with an invisible glass of water. He then did a pantomime of dropping a pill into *hot*—his hands made steam—water, putting the towel over the head and sniff, sniff.

After completely mimed explanations for gargle, sleeping pills, nose drops, and eye drops, they left. Vicki got as far as the car before the laughter exploded.

"What's so damned funny?"

She tried to stifle the mirth, but it kept hiccuping up. It took another hour to get the prescription filled and be on their way. Despite all Vicki's protestations, they took off for Zermatt with Mr. Hyde behind the wheel.

They had to park at Täsch, four miles below Zermatt, which was not accessible by car. Joe pulled into a parking space and leaned back, rubbing his head. Vicki touched his forehead. It felt slightly hot. "Honey, are you sure you're up to the train ride?"

"Yes! We've looked forward to riding the train, and we'll ride the train!"

"Yes, dear." Tread gently through the brambles, she counseled herself. "Did you put the things you need in the small bag?"

"Oh, hell, I forgot."

"Joe, we can't lug that big suitcase with us."

"Well, big deal. I'll just shove a few things into your bag. What can we need, anyway?"

He yanked a few garments out of the suitcase and shoved them into her duffel. Vicki did spot his toiletry case in time for that to be included. They got on the train in strained silence.

The train seemed to Vicki to be going straight up at the same time it dangled over nothing. She had a hard time getting words past her heart, which was lodged in her mouth. "I'm glad the Swiss made this train."

"Why?"

"Because they wouldn't *allow* it to break down." Even the uneasiness between them couldn't eclipse the splendor of the view. The Swiss Alps made all the other mountains look insignificant. She leaned back and started to relax, but the silence was shattered by Joe's fit of sneezing. "How are you doing, hon?" She reached over to lay a consoling hand on his arm.

"Terrible. Vicki, I'm sorry to spoil this. We've looked forward to seeing this for such a long time, and I have to get a lousy cold!"

"It's not your fault, you know."

"I know. It's just such a letdown. Look at that—all that beauty, and what I really want is to be at home in bed."

"*Our* home? In *our* bed?"

"Yes."

She couldn't agree more. Even looking around at all this splendor, she couldn't agree more. That's where she'd like to be, too.

The pressure didn't let up. When they arrived, there wasn't a public conveyance in sight, so they followed the vague instructions they got from a passerby. They finally arrived at a large hotel at the edge of town. By the time they reached the desk, Joe looked as if he was going to pass out, so Vicki took over. "We're Mr. and Mrs. Josef Beck. I believe we have reservations."

The clerk scanned the book. "I can't seem to find your name."

"I need to lie down," Joe moaned.

"My husband is sick. Do you have a room? We can look for the reservations later."

"Well, we do have a small room on the side . . ."

"Fine. We'll take it."

"All right, but it . . ."

Vicki signed the register quickly, before he could back out. Grabbing the duffel bag she said, "We'll just go up. This is our only luggage, so I can manage. Which way is it?"

The room was tiny, with twin beds squeezed together,

but it did have a bath, and there was a beautiful church spire that rose directly across from their open window. Beyond that they could see the Matterhorn. "Oh, Joe, look! The room is cramped, but the view is lovely!"

"As long as there's a bed."

"Oh, yes, honey, you lie down. Do you want a glass of water for your pill?"

"Do you remember which one I'm supposed to swallow?"

"Yes." She gave him the pill and the water, settled him on the bed with a blanket over him, since he didn't even have the energy to undress, then went in to unpack her toiletries case. She was looking forward to a hot bath and a shampoo.

Suddenly the silence was shattered by a cacophonous *bong, bong, bong, bong*. The whole room shook. She raced back to the bedroom in time to see Joe shoot upright, his eyes wide with incredulous horror. "Oh, my Lord! It's that church steeple. It has a gong in it!" It not only had a gong; it also had chimes, which proceeded to ring out, for all the town to hear, a joyous, three-minute-long hymn, while Joe huddled, quivering, under four pillows.

When the silence was restored, Vicki sat on the edge of his bed. "Maybe I should go downstairs and try to get us moved."

"You could tell by the way the guy acted that this was the only room he had. I can see why it was available."

"Joe, this must not be the right hotel. Maybe—"

"No, I don't want to move. We have silence for an hour anyway, and maybe the chimes are only once a day, at teatime, or something."

"Honey, this isn't England."

"Well, we can hope. Vicki, I think I'll take a hot bath, then try some of that inhaling stuff to see if I can clear the passages. Could you call room service and get two large bottles of sparkling water? That helps to settle the stomach."

A short while later he emerged from the bath with a towel wrapped around his middle. "Could you toss me a pair of shorts? I washed mine out."

She rummaged through the bag. "Joe, I hate to tell you this, but you didn't pack any underwear."

"Oh, hell. What about running shorts? Did I throw those in?"

"No."

"What am I going to sit in? This towel is wet, and you'll want to use the other one. Do you have anything I can wear?"

"Joe, you can't fit into my bikinis. Oh, wait, these might work."

"Vicki, those are bloomers! Red bloomers, with ruffles!"

"They're the bottoms to my shortie pajamas. But they have an elastic waistband, so I'll bet you could get them on."

After much grumbling and griping and nose blowing and sneezing, Joe sat, partly encased in bright red ruffled bloomers, on the edge of the bed. With a towel over his head, he was leaning over a small bowl full of hot, vapor-emitting water. At that moment, after the briefest of knocks, the door swung open. A bellhop stood, one hand balancing a tray with two bottles of soda water, a container of ice cubes, and two glasses. His eyes were so round with amazement they looked for all the world as though they'd pop right out.

"Oh! *Mon Dieu!* Pardon, pardon!" Never taking his eyes from the apparition on the edge of the bed, he thrust the tray into Vicki's hands and backed hastily out of the room. *"Mon Dieu!"* he repeated as he hastened down the hall.

Vicki, holding on to the tray as tightly as she could, sank to the floor in helpless laughter. She looked up at Joe in her red panties with the towel still suspended above his head. Their eyes met, and Joe started to laugh too—laugh and sneeze, laugh and sneeze. Then, right on the half-hour, the steeple emitted one loud *bong,* and another spritely hymn assailed the quiet.

Joe and Vicki fell over laughing.

8

VICKI DECIDED TO take matters into her own hands. After a quick bath and shampoo, she went downstairs and then headed for the train. She reached the parking lot, got the reservation information and a few other articles out of Joe's suitcase, and returned to the hotel.

Now armed with the proper information, she ran upstairs and cajoled, scolded, and wheedled Joe into action. Once he dressed and she repacked their few belongings, they both retraced her steps down the stairs. The bill was quickly taken care of, and within an hour and a half of her decision to act, they were on their way to the correct hotel, which had a name similar to the one they were in but was blessedly far away from gongs and chimes.

Joe collapsed gratefully into one of the two large double beds and slept away the rest of the day and almost all of Thursday. Vicki was once again a lone traveler in a foreign land.

Sitting in a coffee house by herself, surrounded by cheerful groups of people babbling away happily in German and

French, did nothing to dispel her gloom. Could money buy friends? she wondered. It would sure as heck buy them lots of eager acquaintances, but not a close-knit group of buddies like the one they had at home.

It occurred to her that she had actually looked forward to the step-by-step climb up the ladder Joe wanted to leap directly to the top of. The struggle would be another "together" process, binding them closer, giving them small, steadily progressive advances to celebrate.

She looked down at the indecently lush piece of cake on the plate before her. A piece of cake. Could she have it and eat it, too? Could both of them, she and Joe, thrive on such a rich diet without becoming bloated and puffed up? Would success spoil Vicki and Joe Beck?

Thursday had come and gone with no discussion, and when Joe awoke on Friday morning feeling greatly improved, they quickly pushed aside all other considerations to take the train up still higher to have lunch at the top of Gornergrat. The day was as perfect as a day could be, and the thrill of sitting on the top of one mountain, looking right across at the peak of the Matterhorn, was enough to help mend anyone's health, Vicki decided.

"Vicki?"

"Hmm?" She paused in the middle of taking a bite of her sandwich.

"Does this give you a feeling of sitting on top of the world?"

She looked across at the famous Matterhorn, more magnificent in real life than any of its many celluloid images could portray. "Yes, it does. Maybe we should sing a chorus of the old song by that name."

But Joe was strangely serious, his face set in lines of deep contemplation. When he spoke, his tone reflected the mood. "I like sitting on top. It makes me wonder why anyone would want to deliberately slide back to the bottom."

She put down the sandwich. "We're not talking about mountains anymore, are we."

Joe looked at her, his brilliant eyes as blue as the brilliant, cloudless sky. "No. We're not. I want it, Vicki. I want it all. The challenge, the excitement, the place at the top."

He wanted the cake, the whole thing. "Are you sure you won't get fat?"

His eyes really focused on her, puzzled. "What?"

"Never mind, just a crazy thought." She gazed out over the incredible scene. "Could you really do it that easily, Joe? Say good-bye to your country, to all the people and places that have been so much a part of your life?"

"Vicki, it's not as though we'd be isolated in Austria. You're still thinking about it in terms of the life we've led before. We could get on a plane any time we wanted and go to the States for a visit."

Vicki's stomach took a dramatic lurch. Go to the States for a visit. He was already talking like someone who belonged to another place. "For a visit. We'd never *live* there again." Something rose up and stuck in her throat. "Joe"— it sounded like a cry for help—"that feels so awful inside. Can you understand that at all? I don't want to hold you back, to be a drag of any kind on your future. But oh, it feels so lonely inside to think of never, ever *living* in America again. I just don't know if I could ever think of myself in any other way. I'm afraid I'd always be American inside."

"I'm not asking you to renounce your citizenship. The world has changed, you know. Lots of people live in countries other than their own."

"I know, and I honestly have been trying to shift gears inside. But Joe, there's a difference. In the short time in Geneva I felt the difference. Like the night we had dinner at the Hôtel du Rhône—remember? We commented on how many different languages were being spoken around us. I got the immediate impression that an American could live in Geneva and still be an American. But Austria... well, Austria seems so thoroughly populated by Austrians!"

He was staring straight ahead, his eyes fixed on the distant snow-topped peak. "That's a brilliant deduction." The comment dripped with sarcasm. When had sarcasm invaded his tone? She couldn't remember ever hearing it there before.

"You know what I mean."

"No, I'm not sure at all what you mean." When his gaze swung to her it was full of bewildered anger. "Vicki, are you telling me that you'd rather go back and live in our cramped little box stall in Cambridge, Mass., U.S.A., and watch me scratch my way up some overcrowded corporate ladder, anxiously awaiting my next review and twenty-dollar raise, than live in a beautiful house in Salzburg and have the entire world at our disposal?"

She had to admit that, put like that, it sounded pretty silly. But the problem was they weren't addressing an issue that could be decided on a strictly logical basis. They were talking about gut-feeling issues, as close to the emotional bone as you could get. They were talking about love—or at least she was. She loved her country, deeply, intuitively, and it was far from easy to bid a permanent good-bye to that kind of love.

They were startled by a deep-timbred voice saying "Excuse me." A big, barrel-chested man stood before them. "I hate to intrude but there are no more tables left. Would you mind if my wife and I shared yours?"

They cast an uneasy glance at each other. Of course they minded, but what could they say? "Please sit down. It's a perfect spot for enjoying the view." Vicki hoped she sounded friendlier than she felt.

The man waved to his wife, a petite woman with ash-blond hair and a hesitant manner. She's embarrassed about intruding, Vicki thought, and she smiled a bit more sincerely.

"Thank you so much. What luck to run into other Americans. It's so nice to hear our native accent now and then. I'm Frank Luigi, and this is my wife Annette."

"Nice to meet you. I'm Joe Beck, and my wife, Vicki."

"Isn't this an incredible view?" Annette's smile was warm. "We come here whenever Frank has enough free time to relax for a few days. Have you been here before?"

"No, it's our first visit." Joe was pulling his amiability into place. "Where do you live? Do you come all the way from the States to admire the mountain?"

Frank laughed. "No, I'm afraid we're not doing quite well enough for that! Right now we're in Zurich. I'm with the opera company there."

"A singer!" Vicki looked at him with new interest. "You have to be a basso."

"You guessed it. Pretty apparent, eh? No disguising the deep tone."

"And then of course you're built a little like a string bass!" Annette took a playful poke at his huge chest, and they laughed. Their playful, familiar air caused Vicki a sharp pang of jealousy.

"How do you like living in Switzerland?" she asked. Pretty apparent what's on your mind, Vicki old girl, she thought.

"It's great! Switzerland is a wonderful country!" Frank Luigi's huge voice matched his huge chest. "So are Italy and France, where we also lived for a while. It's still difficult, you know, for an opera singer to start from scratch and grow into the big roles in our own country. So, we put in our 'foreign service' and wait for the name to grow to match the chest!" The mutual laughter again.

"How long have you been living abroad?" Joe was clearly pleased by their positive demeanor.

"Five years, four months, and twenty-three days," the answer snapped back instantly from Annette.

"Well, it hasn't exactly slipped your mind," Joe observed. Wariness replaced pleasure on his face.

"It's hard to be away from your own country," Frank admitted. "If we could afford to go home more often, I suppose it would help. And I'm lucky that my wife agreed to wait it out with me. But at least the end is in sight. I've been offered two roles in the States next season. If I succeed there, I'll be on my way, and we can go home to stay!"

An uneasy glance passed between Joe and Vicki, but the conversation quickly dispelled the discomfort. The Luigis were delightful, entertaining people and, as Frank said, it was good to talk to Americans. They struck up such a rapport that they all made plans to meet at one of the Luigis' favorite restaurants in Zermatt for dinner.

They rode down in the train together and parted to go to their separate hotels to clean up. Joe and Vicki took showers and short naps and then dressed for dinner without mentioning the touchy subject that was clouding the air.

They had a lovely time with the Luigis. Both Joe and Vicki shared a love of opera, along with many other loves, so all Frank's tales were highly entertaining. Annette was a scenery designer, as busy and involved as he, and her tales of backstage peccadilloes were hilarious. It was fun and gay and nice to see Joe back in good fettle.

They got back to their room late and fell asleep the moment they hit the pillows.

They awoke late the next morning and had to rush to get to the dining room before breakfast hours ended. As soon as they finished the meal, they went back to the room to pack. The weather was a little overcast, the mood a little subdued. It was Saturday morning, and they had to get back to Geneva to catch an evening flight to Salzburg. And their Thursday discussion that had taken place on Friday hadn't solved a thing.

Vicki followed Joe to the elevator, thinking about the Luigis, in particular about Frank's statement that it was hard to live outside your own country. The sentiment had been soundly seconded by his wife. She and Joe hadn't discussed their own situation with the other couple, but had simply told them that Joe was just out of school and considering a job.

"That's an exciting point in life," Annette had commented. "And it's so good that you have your own career, Vicki. I think the one thing that's kept me going all this time is that my own work is so engrossing. And aren't Frank and I lucky to be in the same field? It's always more satisfying to work together!"

And what would I do every day, day after day, in Austria?

The question had been asked before but not answered. The Luigis were so happy at the prospect of going home after all these years. She didn't blame them. The desire to go home was growing in her after only two short weeks. Damn. Her problem was that she was too simple a person. She just wasn't equipped with compulsive desires. She wanted a home and family and friends and time with Joe. Simple? It should be. But it wasn't.

Since Joe's headache was back, Vicki drove from Täsch toward Geneva while he dozed. She was delighted to find a radio station that was playing operatic arias. Someday maybe she'd hear Frank Luigi, she thought. She drove at a leisurely speed. They had plenty of time, and she was in no hurry to hasten the return to Austria. Her mind felt like a small container of clutter and debris, with no order to be found. There was an enormous question waiting for them in Austria, and what in heaven's name was the answer to be?

Vicki leaned back in the plane seat. She loved the feeling of takeoff, the surge of power in the engines, the clunk as the landing gear lifted. It still seemed a miracle to her, this intrusion of humanity into the sky. No wonder she was having trouble adapting to the idea of moving halfway across the world to a new culture. She had a horse-and-buggy mind-set in a jet-travel age.

"Vicki?"

She turned to look at Joe's wonderful, smiling face. "I thought you'd already dozed off. Are you feeling better?"

Joe stretched and readjusted his seat belt. "Yes. In fact I think this cold is just about whipped. I'm sorry it had to foul up part of our vacation. I guess I am sort of a sorehead when I'm sick, aren't I?"

She grinned at him. "Scratch *sort of* and you've got it."

"At least we got to see the Matterhorn, and meeting Frank and Annette was fun."

"Yes."

"We didn't get much settled, did we."

"I don't think we got *anything* settled. Joe, what are you going to tell Anton?"

"I don't know." He leaned his head back against the seat and closed his eyes again, visibly retreating.

"For one thing, Joe, where would we live? It's fine to be a visitor in Anton's upstairs apartment, but on a permanent basis? It would be like living in each other's back pockets."

"Don't you like Anton?"

"Of course I like Anton. What's not to like? He's charming and generous and sweet. I just happen to think that a marriage relationship should consist of two, rather than three, people."

"Are you sure you're not just looking for excuses to say no?"

"Excuses?" She stared at him, then glanced around nervously, aware that her voice had risen. "Since when do I need an excuse? I assumed we were still dealing with freely agreed upon mutual choice!"

He ran his hand across his eyes. "We are. You're right. I don't know why I'm snapping at you. Guess the head isn't completely normal yet. Maybe I'll snooze the rest of the way."

Joe, Joe, don't do this. Don't back away from this discussion. You're leaving me dangling on a broken limb! Why didn't she say it aloud instead of to herself? Because she didn't know how much more of this dreadful feeling of pulling apart she could handle at this moment. She wished she could fall asleep for about five days. A thought hit her with alarming force. And then what? What was going to happen in five days? The return home was no longer on automatic; the gears had been shifted.

Anton met them at the airport alone this time. He was clearly delighted to see them and made a ceremony of helping Vicki into the front seat. He's recognized his stumbling block, she thought. He surprised them by turning left instead of right on the main highway. "We go to Salzburg," he said in a lilting voice. "I wish to display to you something." He then turned the conversation to questions about their trip.

Although he was obviously trying hard to stick to English, it became necessary for Joe to switch to German to relate the complete story of their evening at the strip show in Geneva and the gongs and chimes in Zermatt. By the time Joe had finished, Anton was laughing so hard he had to pull the car to the side of the road. "Ah, ah!" He dabbed at his eyes with his handkerchief. "So funny! You must be having much laughs!"

They had been following the river for a short time when Anton swung into a side street and parked in front of a hotel. "Come, we go inside."

Vicki and Joe exchanged quizzical looks, then followed his uncle. After a brief consultation at the desk, Anton motioned them to come, and they took the elevator to the fourth floor. He led them down the hall and opened one of the doors. With growing curiosity, Vicki went into the room.

"This hotel, it has the living compartments," Anton explained. "Is most nice." He led them through the large, lovely living room to the balcony that ran its length. The view was magnificent. "You see, since we are being on the right banking of the River Salzach, you see most clearly the fortress and much the beauty of our Salzburg." He winked at Vicki. "Is gorgeous, yes?"

"It's certainly gorgeous," she agreed.

He took them through the rest of the apartment. "It is having two bed chambers and also the two baths. And"— they entered a small but cheery and well-appointed kitchen— "the cooking room." They were both too mystified to do anything but look and listen. Once again following his lead, they sat in the living room and watched him expectantly.

"You see, since you are gone, I am doing the thinking. Maybe Joe and Victoria are needing the privacy. So, you have the . . ." With a helpless shrug he said a German word to Joe, who provided the translation. "Ah, yes, the alternative. You might have this, or you might live on the top of my house, or"—a wave of his hand—"many others the possibilities."

Joe's glance swept to Vicki's and locked. He could read the near-panic in her eyes, could feel her vulnerability grow as the negatives were turned to positives. He was glad their discussion about living arrangements had taken place on the plane. At least there was no way she could think he'd alerted his uncle to that problem. Anton's perceptiveness amazed him. It seemed he could anticipate difficulties and move to overcome them before they got started. What was Vicki thinking? She looked flustered and a little angry.

Joe stood and went back to the balcony. What a place to live! So close to this vital and fascinating city. If only Vicki could conquer her fears about moving, it seemed to him this should be infinitely appealing to her, with her love of music and art. He turned and looked in at Anton and Vicki, holding a polite conversation, looking a little stiff and uncertain with each other. He wished Vicki spoke German so she could discover the depth of Anton's unique personality. He wished . . .

He turned around once more, finding the view of the spectacular city easier to deal with than the view of his wife. That thought stopped him cold, making his chest tighten with alarm. Never, since he'd first seen Vicki, had he *not* wanted to look at her. What was happening to them, to the miracle of their love? It had been so great, the time in Geneva—as Anton said, "so much laughs." He and Vicki always seemed to find humor in the same things, to be touched by the same things.

"Joe?" He turned sharply, startled. Anton was standing at the French door. "Are you ready?"

"Yes." He dropped behind, watching Anton's straight back and Vicki's softly curved form. They looked good walking together. He and Vicki must look much the same. Joe was like his uncle—tall and strong. And he wanted to be more like him—sure of himself, sure of his ability and his judgment. As they entered the lobby and Anton returned the key to the desk clerk, Joe observed the hotel staff's eagerness to please Anton. The lure of power and money. It was temptation enough for any man. And add to that the incredible challenge of learning how to run an immense corporation, and of doing it well!

Joe watched Vicki with growing distress the rest of that evening and the following day. She was painfully polite, smiling at all the right times, participating in the conversation, even adding snatches of humor now and then. But to Joe, who knew her every mood, she was remote and uncommunicative. Then on Sunday night she began to sneeze.

"Oh, hell!" she muttered, slamming the empty tissue box down on the bureau. "Now what am I supposed to blow my stupid nose on?"

Joe went into the bathroom and found a fresh box. "Here you are, love. Your nose is rescued." He leaned against the doorjamb. "I thought *I* was the one who got into a foul temper when I got a cold!"

"Well, you don't have a monopoly on foul tempers, you know!"

"Obviously not."

Vicki blew her nose loudly, then went to the closet, where she impatiently rummaged through her few dresses. "I don't know why we have to dress up all the time. Why can't we eat hamburgers and wear our jeans for once?"

"Maybe we can. Shall I ask Anton?"

"Why can't we eat hamburgers and wear jeans up here alone, for once?"

"Vicki..."

"I know, I know, I'm being a pain." She sat down heavily on the bed. "I feel rotten."

"Honey." Joe went to her, putting a consoling hand on her shoulder. "Why not climb into bed and let me bring up a tray? I'll bring one for myself, too. It may not be hamburgers, but we'll be alone. I'm sure Anton would understand."

She plumped up a couple of fat down pillows and eased back against them. "Joe, to tell you the truth, what I'd really like is a bowl of soup, followed closely by sleep. So don't cancel your meal with Anton. He gets so much pleasure from your company, and I'm in no condition to get pleasure from anything but temporary oblivion."

"I'm sorry." He sat beside her. "You know, all I've ever wanted to give you is joy, and now I seem to be giving you not only a passel of problems but a cold to boot."

He got a weak, watery smile. "The cold I can live through."

Her reply sobered him. "We can live through the rest, too, Vicki. We'll work it out. After all, it's not as if we've been threatened with the plague—just with wealth, position, and success."

"Joe, dammit! I wish you'd stop making it sound so simple! You know damn good and well that if your uncle's wonder-company were in *any* state of the union, my advice to you would be to sign on the dotted line before he had a chance to change his mind. And the comparison you made when we were at Gornergrat, about accepting this versus returning to the little apartment in Cambridge, is unfair, and you know it! You've already had job offers that would excite any other man in the middle of his career. And the only reason we lived so frugally anyway was so your education would be paid for on an as-you-go basis. So don't give me the it's-this-or-poverty routine, because I don't buy it!"

She scrunched down deeper in the pillows. "On second thought, never mind the hot soup. Just see if somewhere among the vintage wine you can discover a bottle of good old scotch, and mix some with ice cubes and soda water— excuse me, sparkling water. Better still, send out for some Appalachian corn mash special. I'm sure it could be flown in by tomorrow."

Joe almost backed out the door. He'd better beat a fast retreat. When Vicki used two *damns* in one statement things were getting hot and heavy. He had to concede the point. She was undoubtedly right that he could get a better than average job in the States. Joe wasn't vain, but he was realistic enough to recognize his ability. He had been called brilliant so many times in his life that most of the time the term rolled over him unnoticed.

He closed the door behind him as he stepped into the

hall, then, halfway down the ornately carpeted steps, he sat down. He was suddenly weighted down with the enormity of what they were dealing with.

It was all very well for him to keep slamming at Vicki about accepting Anton's offer, but had he really thought it through? What if she said no? His head sank in his hands. He had mentally latched on to this opportunity with the same compulsion with which he'd pursued his master's degree. Single-minded, unbending.

Many of his friends had thought him nuts to put up with so much hardship. He recalled a conversation with Bud Sears, a college buddy. "What the hell are you putting yourself through all this for, Joe?" he had demanded. "You and Vicki both—you're out of your tree! You could have a great job right now, without any further schooling. Or if you're that determined—a guy with your brains?—you could get a loan and pay it back later. You're sure to make good money someday. Or you could sign on with a company and let them pay the freight. About all you'd have to do is agree to stay with them for five years or so."

But Joe hadn't wanted to be indebted. Not to a bank, not to a company. But he was indebted. To a lovely woman who was lying in bed upstairs with a cold. That *he* had given her. "Here, hon, as a little thank-you gift for all your help, support, love, and constant, unbending devotion..." He stood up abruptly and finished the trek down the stairs.

When Anton heard about Vicki's condition and her request for a drink, he set to work with a vengeance. Joe watched with a mixture of fascination and horror as his uncle poured at least three jiggers of scotch into a small pan, followed by a cupful of rich, dairy-fresh milk, a large dollop of honey, some dried herbs, and to top it off, a generous dash of schnapps. This he heated on the stove while Louisa stood by, shaking her head, and Joe stood by, wondering if his wife would survive the cure.

When a solicitous Anton carried the creation up to Vicki, she sniffed it apprehensively and asked, "What's in it?"

"You don't want to know," Joe answered.

"Drink! Drink! Is good for the health!"

Vicki took a tentative sip. "Hey, it's good."

While Joe watched, enthralled, she slowly downed the whole thing. No doubt about her sleeping tonight!

Once he saw that his concoction was being consumed, Anton disappeared, then came back with an oblong metal box. "Is for the feets. They need the heat!" He took it into the bathroom, filled it with water, and plugged it in. After giving Joe detailed instructions on how long Vicki should soak her feet, he dashed downstairs again.

"What is he, a frustrated doctor?" Vicki asked.

The drink had already mellowed Vicki's mood. Joe wondered how long it would take before it wiped her out.

"Come on, my pretty, we have orders to soak your 'feets.' Is good for the health." He had to offer a fairly sturdy support to get her into the bathroom, where he helped her out of her clothes and into the famous shortie pajamas.

"Ow! That's hot!"

"It's supposed to be hot."

"Is this instead of the rack and the iron maiden, or is it really supposed to do something good for me?"

"I don't know, but Mom always made me soak my feet when I had a cold as a kid."

"Oooh, what was in that drink? I have a feeling that by morning I may use this to soak my head."

"That drink will either kill you or cure you."

"Great, thanks a lot. Just what I've always wanted to be: someone's guinea pig."

Vicki didn't make the prescribed fifteen-minute foot soak. She swore that her feet were parboiled and went back to collapse in bed. "Joe?"

"What, honey?"

"I'm afraid it's going to be kill."

"Uh-oh."

At that moment Anton reappeared, armed with a thermos pitcher. "Here is the herb tea. Is good for the health. You drink it all night. You run out, Joe can make more, yes?" He bustled around Vicki, offering more pillows, promising that tomorrow they would go to "the chemist" and get some "medicines."

Sinking rapidly into her wished-for oblivion, Vicki muttered, "G'night." Joe and Anton, two now-superfluous males, tiptoed out to let her sleep.

The next day, true to his word, Anton postponed his departure for work long enough to make a trip to the chemist. When he returned, he was armed with more medicines than Joe had been given in Montreux. It was Vicki's turn to swallow, sniff, and gargle, as well as soak her feet.

"This is a dangerous place to get sick," she moaned to Joe. "I have more cures here than there are diseases."

Although Joe offered, with Anton's support, to stay at home with Vicki on Monday, she insisted that he accompany Anton to work. She knew he wanted to go, and she also knew he would sleep most of the day.

It was a decision she was to regret in the three days to follow, for it set a pattern that stuck like glue. She was solicitously watched over by Louisa and Sophie, the cleaning woman, and Anton and Joe called her several times a day to check on her progress. No one could have had better care, but the loneliness grew as her health improved. Joe came home each evening full of stories, his face a pleasure-beam of excitement, and she felt more and more cut off from the man she loved.

And then the evening before their scheduled departure was upon them, and the handwriting was on the wall. Anton wanted them to extend their stay. She could probably get Joe out of there—if she had a few sticks of dynamite—but his preference was clear. He had the bit in his teeth, and he was off and running. Vicki, recovered in body but still flagging in spirit, listened to the patient explanations that both Anton and Joe gave her at dinner. There was no need to hurry home—did Joe still think about it as home, or had that simply become an expression? Vicki wasn't due to start work for another week, and Joe had no immediate commitments . . .

Vicki drank the last of her after-dinner tea, which Anton had assured her was better for the health than coffee while she was still recuperating, and stood. "I'd like to go upstairs and think this through. I need to figure out what I have to get done before my actual appointments begin. It's important, at least to me, and I haven't had a chance to give it a moment's thought." Joe started to follow her, but she encouraged him to stay for the schnapps. "It would be more productive for me to outline my upcoming schedule first, so I know what I'm doing."

Her upcoming schedule was perfectly laid out already; she'd taken care of that before she left. But she did need the time alone. As she sat in the dark in the upstairs apartment on one of the downy soft chairs with the snow-white upholstery, looking out at the black sky so crammed full of twinkling stars, she knew beyond question what she had to do.

She had to go home. For how long, she had no idea. She also had no idea what her ultimate decision would be. But the little I-want-to-go-home girl inside her held her heart in her hands as surely as the little marble girl in Anton's front hall held the kitten. And she knew something else, too. As surely as she must go home tomorrow, Joe must stay.

When Joe came upstairs, he was appalled to see that Vicki had packed her suitcase. "What are you doing? Vicki, I don't think it's fair for you to just arbitrarily decide that we're going without even asking what I want to do."

She turned to him, her face a mask of concealed emotions. "I already know what you want to do, Joe. And I know what I want to do."

A hot surge of alarm coursed through him. "You're not saying . . ."

"No." She hurried to him, putting her arms around his waist and leaning her head on his chest. It felt so familiar and so good. "I'm not suggesting anything permanent or even long-term. But I have to attend to my patients. They're only children, Joe, and they get upset if I'm not there when

I'm expected. And there are things to arrange before the schedule starts." She stopped, then looked up at him, her eyes swimming. "Oh, let's be honest, honey. We're both confused. I can't sort out anything here. There's too much subtle pressure. You and Anton both watching my every reaction, catering to my every desire. I'm not used to all this attention."

"But, Vicki, honey, I can't get along without you."

"It won't be long, Joe. And whatever happens, I'm sure that once you go to work there'll be short separations. Don't most businessmen travel?"

He sank onto the bedside chair, his legs suddenly weak and his temples throbbing. "Vicki, I don't think this is a good idea."

"All right then, what do you suggest?"

They looked helplessly at each other, caught in a web, neither having any clue as to how to escape. Joe rubbed his fingers over his throbbing temples. "Couldn't you call home, have someone fill in for you for a while? You haven't really given this a lot of time."

She pulled up the other chair and sat facing him. Two negotiators without a bargaining table. "Joe"—her voice was choked, shaken—"if I stay now and let my work fall behind, I'll get resentful. If you come home now, without having time to fully study what you'd be doing here, you'd be resentful. Our problem is a biggie. Right now we're in a no-win situation. Neither one of us can afford to make our decision solely on the basis of what the other wants without creating instant martyrdom."

"Vicki, I can't do this unless we at least have a timetable on it."

"Okay. What do you suggest?"

"A week?"

"That may not be quite enough, honey. I want to go see my parents. I thought I might stay there for five or six days. For some reason I want to be with them for a while. I might even try to visit my new nephew. Why don't we say two weeks? That'll give both of us time to think on our own.

Then we'll be much better prepared to put our heads together."

"Then what?"

"What do you mean?"

"Will you come back here, or do I come home?"

She hesitated, then decided not to ask him what *home* meant to him right now. After all, that was one of the things he had to decide, just as she did. "Well, I'll be back at work by then, but if you think Anton will spring for another plane ticket, I'll get a substitute for a few days and come for a long weekend." She saw the expression on his face and added, "Or, depending on what it looks like the decision will be from our telephone conversations and all, I'll start looking for a permanent replacement. But Joe . . ."

"What?"

"Don't count on it. I'm not making any promises. I can't. Not yet."

He looked ashen. "The hell of it is, neither can I."

"I know."

They went to bed, but they didn't make love. They just held each other very tightly.

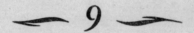

9

VICKI SAT ON an old-fashioned glider on the old-fashioned covered porch that ran across the front of her parents' large, old-fashioned house in Ohio. The house—one of a compatible row of comfortable, rambling homes—stood on a wide street that was well shaded by big trees, many of which had been there even longer than the houses.

She pushed the glider back and forth, enjoying the familiar squeak of its aging springs. Familiar. It was all so familiar, and she enjoyed all of it. The kids riding up and down the street on their bikes, hollering back and forth in good old English; the two shaggy dogs of doubtful ancestry that leaped and barked around them—all were so reminiscent of her childhood years.

She felt whole again, integrated into the society that had spawned her, nurtured her, and helped her to grow into what she hoped was a mature, well-adjusted individual. She heard the comforting voices of her mom and dad calling back and forth to each other from separate rooms in the house.

Her father still ran the local drugstore. He was not only the pharmacist, but often a substitute diagnostician for those

141

locals who still believed that their friend behind the drug counter was more reliable than that new young upstart of a doctor in town. When her father learned she was coming home for a few days, he had arranged to take some time off to be with his daughter.

"Hey, Billy!" One of the boys had stopped his bike in front of the house. "Let's go to the circle and play kick-the-can!"

Kick-the-can! She didn't believe it. Her dad had taught her and her sisters and brother and all their accumulated friends how to play it when they were little. He had referred to the game as a relic of a bygone era then! Yet these kids were going to play it now! She had to force herself to stay in the glider instead of running after them to see if she could play, too.

"Vicki, how are you doing? Your mother is just putting that apple pie in the oven. I hope you're not on one of your diets."

She looked up into the dear, kindly, weathered face of her father. "Dad, have you ever known me to have the willpower to pass up Mom's pie?"

"Now that you mention it, no."

"Let me assure you, I'm not about to break any records now."

He sat beside her on the glider, adding greater dimension to the comfort of her surroundings.

"Dad, would you believe that the neighborhood kids are going down to the circle to play kick-the-can?"

"Is that right? They must have decided they liked it after all."

She turned to him. "You mean *you* taught them?"

"Now come on, don't sound so surprised. I'm still fully capable of delivering a good solid kick to a tin can!"

Vicki laughed. "I didn't mean to insinuate that you weren't. I'm just surprised that you're still acting as neighborhood sports coach."

"Well, that would be exaggerating a little. The truth is that all the kids stop by—oh, almost every weekend—for some of your mom's cookies, and I just happened to mention the game. They all seemed to want to give it a try, so . . . the rest is history."

"Do you know how good this feels, Dad? To sit on this old glider and breathe in that wonderful smell of newly cut grass and listen to the kids playing and the neighbors chatting over the fence next door? It's all so . . . American. And better still, it's all in English."

"Vicki, what are you going to do about Joe and his uncle and Austria?"

"Oh, Dad, I don't know. Do you have any good advice?"

He patted her knee. "No, and I wouldn't give it if I did. This is between you and your husband. Naturally it would be hard for your mother and me, and I'm sure for your sisters and brother, having you so far away. I don't say that to add any pressures. You already know we'd miss you. But we have always, first and foremost, wanted the best for you, Vicki. And I guess that's what you're trying to decide: what's best."

She shifted her position, tucking her feet under her. "I'm not sure I'm even dealing with *best,* Dad. I think I'm still on *possible.*"

"I'm not sure I follow you."

"I don't know if it's *possible* for me to move to Austria. It's so strange. You know me—I've never been one to shy away from the better things in life, but this has such an enormous emotional price tag."

"I'm still not sure I follow you."

The screen door banged as her mother came out to join them.

"Here, Madge, have this seat."

"No, no. Sit. I'll just pull up this chair."

Vicki gazed at her mother for a moment, noticing that her hair was grayer, hating the signs of encroaching age. She wanted both of them to stay as they were forever. "Oh, Mom, that pie smells marvelous." She smiled. "Mom, apple pie . . ." She looked up at the bare flagpole. "Where's the American flag?"

Her father grinned at her. "We can run it up if it'll make you feel better."

"No, don't bother." She was struggling to keep her emotions under control. As usual, her parents sensed her mood.

Her mother's face was worried. "Vicki, why don't you just let it out. We know you're unhappy."

"Oh, Mom . . . Dad!" When the tears were released, they flowed out in a torrent. "I'm so frightened!"

Her father put his arms around her, offering incredible comfort still, after all these years. "Cry it out, honey, cry it out. Then we can talk about it."

She let the flood run, then subside, at its own speed. Then she told her parents, in far more detail than they'd had time for up till now, what the situation was. "I know Joe thinks I'm foolish for not wanting to move. But it isn't something I can explain rationally. I *know* it's an unbelievable opportunity—I'm not dense—it's just . . ." She looked from one beloved face to the other. "I don't know; maybe it's this . . ." She waved her hand to encompass the house and the street. "I grew up believing in God first, America second, and family third. Living in another country for a year, even a few years, might sound like an exciting adventure. But forever? That's exile!"

The worried look didn't fade from her mother's face. "I can understand that, Vicki. I honestly can. I'm afraid I'd feel the same way. Oh, dear! I hope we didn't raise you to be too provincial for today's world."

"Mom, believe me, there's no way you could have prepared me for the stratum Anton Beck lives on. It's unreal. Even without the main issue, which is location, I have to confess that moving up to that level without any chance to adjust to the height is scary." She cast another plaintive glance around. "This has forced me to come to grips with so many things that I don't think most people ever have to face—like how much wealth can you really handle? I guess, under all my extravagant daydreams, what I've always wanted, or at least assumed I'd have someday, is something like this—a nice home in a nice neighborhood. Working my way up in my profession while my husband did the same in his. Maybe a couple of kids. Getting excited about buying a new car. Getting ecstatic over buying a first little house." She clasped her hands and pushed them between her knees. "Ye gods, listen to me. I sound like Cinderella refusing to move up the hill to the castle."

Her father was tapping his fingers on his knee. Vicki watched him for a minute, then said. "Okay, Dad, what is it?" She and her mother exchanged glances and laughed. It was his well-known weigh-it-before-you-say-it gesture.

"Well, I was recalling a conversation your mother and I had with you when you first told us you were going to marry Joe."

Vicki stared at him, a slow recollection coming to her. "Oh, my gosh. I bet I remember it. I'd forgotten all about it."

"We figured as much. It was pretty obvious at the time that you thought we were—what was your expression? Oh yes—'off the wall.' As you may now recall, it was our one and only reservation about your marriage. Joe is one of the finest young men I've ever known, but as you've said yourself, you're what's called a down-home girl. And Josef Beck is far from a run-of-the-mill, ordinary man."

"But, Dad—"

"Now, Vicki, don't get me wrong. You've always been more than just bright yourself. It doesn't surprise us that you've jumped in there with ease and kept right up with him. You've matched him step by step in his extraordinary determination to get the schooling he thought he needed without owing a plug nickel to anyone. You've not only applauded his academic achievements; you've helped him attain them. And at the same time you've made amazing strides in your own career.

"But in a way, being the strange creatures we all are, sometimes the tough situations are easier, because then your help is needed. Now I can understand your reluctance to move away from this country permanently, because frankly, I just plain couldn't do it. And we know how important your own work is to you, honey, and so does Joe. If he doesn't seem to be paying as much attention to that as he should right now . . . well, I'd say that was a pretty good indication of how much he thinks he wants this job."

"*Thinks* he wants it? Dad, there's no question about how much he wants it!"

"Don't be too sure. Joe doesn't have a lot of shortcomings, but you know he has one. He talks about it himself, and Rudolph reminds him when he forgets." He chuckled at that. He was very fond of Rudolph. "Joe has a sort of tunnel vision, Vicki. When he sets his sights on something, he needs to have other things along the way pointed out to him."

"That's true, Dad. But I'm not sure if I can get his attention right now. Or even if I should."

"Well, now, this uncle of his sounds like another exceptional man. If he knew how strongly you felt about these issues, he just might find a way around them. I don't know, of course, but it would be worth talking to him about. But, Vicki"—the loving face was creased with concern—"while you and Joe have given yourselves some time apart, I strongly advise you to face a fact that I believe you've avoided. You're married to a man who's bound for the top. He knows it; he and I have talked about it. I don't think Joe could avoid success if he wanted to, and he doesn't. He's a great big thick cut above average, and if you're going with him, you'll have to get used to the altitude."

"You did it anyway."

"What?"

"Gave me some good advice."

When Vicki left Ohio to return to Boston, she was strengthened in spirit if not closer to a solution. Joe had called her every evening, and while she'd thrilled to the sound of his voice, she'd had to try hard to stifle the feeling that he just might be climbing the mountain faster without her around to slow him down.

She hadn't even considered, before the discussion with

her folks, the possibility that she wasn't up to being Joe's wife. She knew her father would be appalled to know he had instilled such a thought in her mind, but it was especially difficult to keep the idea from surfacing after a long-distance call from Joe. He sounded so alive, so entranced with the rarefied atmosphere he was in. Her dad was right: There was no way she would settle down on a small-town street in an average neighborhood as Mrs. Josef Beck.

She arrived back at her apartment about five-thirty that afternoon and had no sooner put down her suitcase than the phone rang. She rushed to answer it. "Hello?"

"Hi, honey." He sounded so near. Why did it have to be an illusion? "How was your trip?"

"Just fine. No problems. Mom sent me home with enough cookies and home-baked bread to feed all the hungry in Boston."

"I don't doubt it. If you go to the public green, there's plenty of water to cast it on."

"Very clever." She was finding the light banter next to impossible. She wanted to cry, to scream, to beg him to come home. "How's Anton?"

"Just fine. He sends his love. And your tickets for your flight back here will be mailed to you. I can hardly wait, honey."

"Me either. Joe?"

"Hmm?"

"Does Anton's company have a subsidiary in the United States?"

"Yes. In Hartford, Connecticut. It isn't one of the major offices, however; not where the action is."

Yes, dear, she thought, I get the message.

"Why do you ask?"

You know darn well why I ask, and you just gave me the answer, which is "no way." "I was just curious."

"Vicki, did you find someone to handle your job for you?" She could hear the rest of the question. *And if so, for how long? Two days? Forever?*

"Actually, I just rescheduled so I can have a long weekend—Friday through Monday." She gave a nervous laugh, knowing that Joe would be disappointed there at the other end of this long, long cord. "Friday through Monday is stretching a weekend about as far as it can stretch."

"What about at the end of the weekend?"

"Joe, I don't want to talk about this over the phone. We have four more days. We need to use them to think about *all* the alternatives."

"What does that mean?"

"Just what it sounds like. Joe?"

"Yes?"

"I miss you so much."

"It couldn't possibly be more than I miss you."

As soon as Joe hung up the phone, he went to the door to the balcony and stood, feet planted apart, hands in his back pockets, staring at the massive, all-dominating mountain. "Can't you look like something else for a while?" he snarled at it. "A lake maybe, or a sandy beach? Even a crowded street." Turning back with an impatient movement, he flopped into one of the soft chairs and deliberately put his feet up on the ornate table. "Take that!" he hissed.

Anton had gone to France on business. He had left Joe with the BMW, Louisa to cook for him, and Sophie to clean for him. Joe reached over and took a magazine out of the stand and tossed it onto the floor. "There, now Sophie will have something to do."

What Anton had not left him with were any duties. He didn't know enough about the business to accomplish anything, and Herr Hollweg and Herr Berchtold were both on tight schedules and unable to give him any time. He didn't feel right asking Gretchen for help. He was all too aware of the threat he posed to her, and he hated the feeling he got when he looked into her eyes.

He went to the kitchen and opened the refrigerator door. Maybe a late snack. No, he wasn't hungry. He'd bet anything he knew what Vicki would do. She'd take the MTA into Boston early so she'd have time to sit outside under the awning at Lily's in Quincy Market, and have a hamburger and a spinach salad for dinner. Damn, how he wished he were there with her! That sounded like so much fun. They'd sit there and watch all the people and make up stories about the more interesting characters. Lord, how he missed her.

He moved back to the balcony, slumping into one of the outside chairs, staring vacantly at the same obtrusive mountain. The persistent feeling that kept attempting to worm its way into his consciousness was at it again. It was more than Vicki he missed. Hell. He jumped up and went back to the phone and quickly dialed a number. It rang five times before it was answered. "Yes?"

"Dad?"

"Josef! What a surprise. My, it is good to hear from you again so soon! Nothing is wrong, is it?"

"No, Dad, everything's fine. I just felt like talking. How's Mom? Is she there?"

"No, like I told you yesterday when you phoned, she had a meeting. You know, the flower ladies."

"Oh, that's right, her garden club."

"Yes. Josef, is Vicki there yet?"

"No, not for a few more days."

"And what is Anton doing?"

"He went to Paris on business."

"Ah, so that is it. You're lonely."

"Dad! That's silly. I just wanted to check in, make sure you were okay—you and Mom."

"Josef, don't fool with your father. You're calling more often than you do when you're at home in Massachusetts. Why so adamant? What's wrong with being lonely? If I were away from my Maria for two weeks, I would be crying myself to sleep."

The silence hung over the transcontinental connection. "Dad, what am I going to do?"

"Josef. You haven't asked me a question like that for at least fifteen years. You must be very confused. What does your heart tell you?"

"To be with Vicki."

"Then be with Vicki."

"But how?"

"Find a way."

"That's easier said than done."

"Free advice, as the old saying goes, is worth what you pay for it."

"Thanks, Dad. Good night."

"Good night, Josef. Josef!"

"What?"

"Don't give up what is closest to your heart. The ache will never go away."

"That sounds like advice from a man who knows."

"The closest thing to my heart is your mother. But she and I, we have still the love of our native land. It was necessary to leave, and we have also the love of this country. But the ache... Ah, Josef, the ache, it never leaves."

Joe could feel tears welling in his eyes. "Dad, thank you."

"Good night, Josef."

Joe slouched in the chair by the phone, his emotions tumbling and twisting. Never had his father spoken about his native land in such a way. And the thing that had really shaken Joe was the way it was said. His father's accent had become more pronounced as he spoke of his loss. Loss. What was he about to lose? The nagging mind-intruder was knocking again, demanding entrance.

To hell with this! He would go downstairs and find that bottle of scotch, have a nightcap that was *not* a schnapps, and go to bed. After all, the weekend would bring Vicki. And Vicki would bring... Vicki would bring back his heart.

She was actually in his arms. The wonder of her warmth flowed through him, renewing him, making him breathe freely again. "Vicki."

"Joe. Oh, Joe, I can't believe I'm really with you. I've been so lonely without you."

He looked down at her upturned mouth. Her clover-green eyes were awash with tears. He hoped they were happy tears. He just held her and looked at her, re-memorizing the smooth curve of her cheek, the silky skin that covered those delicate bones, the shining brown curls around her sweet, sweet face. He lowered his mouth to hers . . . Unbelievable, the softness of those lips! He had to tear himself away from her. "I guess we'd better get out of here. I'm about to succumb to my need of you."

She smiled, and his heart turned over. How could he have lived for eleven whole days without seeing that smile? "Where's Anton?"

"Anton is in Paris. He called this morning to say he wouldn't be returning until Sunday. I think he knows how much I wanted to have you to myself."

"Dear Anton. He's such a love. And I'm so glad he's not here."

Joe picked up her suitcase, grinning at her.

When she saw the BMW she paused for just an instant. "Is anything wrong?"

She shook her head. "No. It just seems so strange for us to be getting into a car like this without someone else at the wheel. I guess I had just enough time at home to become accustomed to our banged-up Toyota."

"Would you rather have a banged-up Toyota? I'm sure it could be arranged."

"No, it's all right. I'm willing to sacrifice."

Joe put the car into gear, still thrilled by the powerful roar of the engine as it took off. It was so damned good to have Vicki here, sitting by his side. So good to have their silly-happy dialogue slipping back into place.

All the way to Anton's house Joe had to fight to keep his eyes on the road instead of on Vicki. He continually reached over to touch her, to lay his hand on her arm, to tangle his fingers in her hair, to rest his hand on her leg. Anything to assure himself that she was there, right beside him. They talked about her trip and her visit to Ohio and the fact that she hadn't made it to see young Andy but had talked to Evelyn and Jeffrey on the phone several times. He wanted to hear the sound of her voice. He wanted to shout at the top of his lungs: "I missed you so! Don't ever leave me again! I need you!" He intended to say those things, but later, when he could look into her eyes and let her know how deeply he meant them.

As soon as they were inside their apartment, Joe dropped her bag and they reached for each other hungrily. "Vicki, Vicki. Do you have any idea of the terrible damage that's been done to my well-being by your absence?"

She came into his arms readily, her supple, slim body bending into his, pressing against the rapidly expanding evidence of his need. "Joe, I want you so much. How fast can you take those clothes off?"

"Just watch."

They stood, scarcely inside the front door, pulling their clothes off with careless disregard for their condition, tossing them hastily, not checking to see where they landed.

When Joe was naked he reached out to help Vicki unfasten her bra and pull down her panties. Then he held himself away from her in order to savor the sight of each and every curve, of the flawless skin, of the round, tempting breasts with their inviting, kiss-pink tips. He lifted his hand and slowly, tenderly, ran it over her shoulder, down her arm, letting it shift to the small waist and settle for just a moment. He felt a shiver of pleasure run through him. There was nothing, nothing that felt as good as Vicki's skin.

"Vicki." He took her hand and led her to the middle of the room to a spot right under one of the huge skylights. "I want the best light possible so I can see every inch of you."

Her slim, creamy-smooth hands touched his chest, palms flattening out to glide gently over the hairy surface. How could someone's touch cause such delight?

"Joe," she whispered.

He felt a groan building within him as her hands slid down over his flat stomach, her fingers tracing the hip bones, down, down to cup him, to hold his aching need in their grasp.

His fingers closed around her tiny wrists, imprisoning them in a mini-lock of love, exerting pressure so the two of them sank together to the floor. The blazing sunlight skimmed and flickered over her dampening skin, giving it the visual illusion of flesh-colored velvet. Joe kissed her, his hot, seeking lips capturing hers, sucking them in, touching them with his tongue. He wanted to devour her, to ingest the substance of her. His tongue thrust into her opening mouth, twirling, dancing with hers, his mind registering *delicious, delicious, delicious*. Lowering his head, he took one ripe, taut nipple into his mouth, sucking on it greedily, savoring it.

Vicki trembled, her whole being responding with quivering urgency to this reawakened, reborn celebration of their love. She could feel her spine curving forward, pressing her tingling nipple deeper into his mouth, her hips curling in toward his searching fingers. Her blood was bubbling, a lava stream of fiery force, carrying the heat-pricks of desire to her toes, to the tips of her fingers, flicking across the backs of her eyes, making them tense more tightly closed. Was it possible for this to go on, or would she explode into shimmering fragments of desire?

They took their time with their lovemaking, touching, tasting, exploring each other's bodies with rapacious thoroughness. Vicki lay back, letting him trace her curves with his minutely questing hands, letting herself be nipped, tasted, licked everywhere like a sugary lollipop. Then she retraced every bit of Joe's familiar body, wanting to assure herself that all of him was still the same—smell, taste, feel, response.

They goaded each other to the brink of ecstasy once, again, and yet again, backing off, not willing to have it end. But Vicki could feel the hot-licking tentacles spreading, engulfing, pushing her closer and closer. "Joe!"

"I'm coming, oh baby, I'm coming to you." He thrust into her with hard, almost brutal force, just barely satisfying her need for a turbulent union. They pushed into each other as though they could bury themselves in the other's skin, and, clasped together, they rolled over and over, a white-hot wheel singeing the carpet.

They cried out at the same time, their calls of fulfillment bouncing around the walls, encircling them in another love wheel.

"Vicki, my darling, darling Vicki. Don't every ever leave me again." He held her to him, loath to let her go, afraid to sever the connection. There was a completeness about him when he was this close to Vicki that he never felt at any other time.

"Joe, how could I forget, in such a short time, how good that feels?"

"It feels that good because we're so very, very right together, and so very wrong apart."

Vicki sat up beside him, her dark curls damp and tumbled, her skin still flushed. "We are wrong apart, aren't we. Off-balance and off-key."

Joe slowly rose to his feet and extended a hand. "Come on, let's take a shower. We can both easily fit into the one in this bathroom."

Vicki laughed aloud for the first time since she left Joe. "Back to bathrooms again! If we ever build a house, I shudder to think what it will look like: probably a small kitchen, one bedroom, and a teeny sitting area, all clustered around four huge bathrooms!" Once more in tune—back on *laughingly*—they went, hand in hand, to take a shower.

After a relaxed lunch, prepared and presented with a flourish by Louisa, who seemed genuinely glad to have her back, Vicki went upstairs to take a nap. She hadn't been able to sleep on the plane, and the trip, along with the cloud of irresolution that hung over them, had worn her out.

That evening they went in to Salzburg for dinner at the Zinnkrug, a lovely restaurant on the right bank of the river. They had a window seat, which allowed a full view of the movie-set spectacle that was Salzburg. Sipping the bubbling champagne Joe had ordered as a celebration, Vicki gazed out over the quiet river and across at the entrancing skyline.

There was no denying its appeal. It looked like an artist's concept of a city built to personify humanity's eternal reverence for beauty. But it was real.

She could feel its spell winding invisible streamers of enticement around her, making her feel part of the past, part of the future, part of its own particular piece of the present. She was being subtly seduced by Salzburg. Ah, but you have a rival, she mentally warned it, a great, noisy, stubbing-its-toes-with-newness country. It's not as smoothed over by time as you, or as rich in history as you, but it's my first love. And you know what they say about first loves.

"Pretty special, isn't it?"

She met Joe's clear blue gaze across the flickering candlelight, struck, as always, by the pleasure of looking at him. "I have just the tiniest little suspicion that you selected this restaurant to remind me of the view from the hotel apartment."

"Such a suspicious nature. I don't know that we ever even discussed the apartment. Did you like it?"

"I thought it would be an absolutely perfect place for two people to live, if they were going to live in Austria."

His gaze dropped. "Do I take it that you're no more positive about that now than you were before you left?"

She made herself keep looking at him, at the top of his bowed, blond head, steeling her reserve, mentally staving off the temptation to gaze out across the river. The moment had come. There was no avoiding the truth that must be spoken, the confrontation that must take place. She spoke in a quiet, steady tone. "It's time, isn't it, for us to face whatever our future is to be."

His eyes once again met hers. "Yes. Why do I get the feeling this isn't going to be pleasant?"

"Because I'm not going to say what you want me to say." She took a fortifying swallow of the champagne. Was this what was called buying time? She'd buy it or rent it or steal it right now. She didn't want to face the inevitable. "I can't just say 'Yes, by all means, I'll come,' and the reasons why aren't going to be easy to explain. How do I tell you, Joe? How do I describe to you what *home* feels like?"

"Vicki, I have to stop you on that for a minute. You've

mentioned it so often. How can you be so sure *this* won't feel like home someday?"

"I can't. Because there's no way of knowing. But if I can hardly deal with what I know to be true today, how can I try to foresee tomorrow? Joe, please, look at me. This is hard for me to say anyway, and I can't say it to the top of your head. I'm not giving you a flat either-or answer. But I have to be honest with you, just as we've always been honest with each other, because ultimately you're the one who has to make the decision about the job. So just let me finish. Then I'll relinquish the floor to you."

"For what—to fall on?"

She let that pass, already struggling with the iron resolve she had mustered in the days before her return. She knew what she was saying was important, but she didn't know if she could make it *sound* important. "Since we don't exactly seem to be on the same wavelength, I'd better just spit it out, and we'll have to deal with it piecemeal. Number one, I can't move away from my country for the rest of my life. I can't imagine doing that without having this sick, sick feeling in my stomach. The one I have right now, just thinking about it."

"This is so hard for me to understand," Joe said. "Look out there at that beautiful city. Think about the kind of life we'd be leading: busy and vital and full of excitement. And we'd be together. Isn't that the most important thing?"

Wasn't it? Wasn't it? The question bounced around in her head, demanding an answer. "Yes," she whispered, searching for her voice. "Yes," she repeated. "The problem is, it isn't the *only* thing. Interesting, exciting, vital? For you, unquestionably. For me? Maybe. After all, Joe, *you're* the one who always reminded me, when I got into a snit about some far-off future thing, that life was a day-to-day business. What's made our daily life such a pleasure? Hard work—together; striving—together; planning our future— together; and spending every spare moment we could muster with our friends, our *mutual* friends.

"And Joe, what about the other great big important issue that you seem more and more to brush aside: What about *my* work? You know how important it is to me, how I'd dreamed of someday, when you were established, going back to school myself."

"Honey, I'm sure you'd be able to find a college near Salzburg that offers classes in English, and you'll learn German faster than you think you will, once you live here." His eyes had brightened again; a possible selling point had been introduced.

"Joe, listen to what I'm saying. It's so important! It isn't the job, it isn't Anton, it isn't even most of the issues we just discussed. I'd take my chances on all of those, just to be sure we'd be together. There's just one immense, over-riding obstacle. It is, and has been, and always will be called *home*. I'd love to live down the street in that charming apartment for a while, even a few years, or part of every year. The German language doesn't scare me anymore; I'm sure I'd learn it quickly enough if I put my mind to it. But Joe, if you tell Anton yes, you're giving him a lifetime commitment. And *I* simply cannot commit myself to living here—in a sense attempting to become Austrian—for the rest of my life."

He was shaking his head in an I-don't-want-to-acknowledge-this gesture. "Where does this leave me?"

She had to duck her head to dab at the tears that insisted on rolling down her cheeks. "I don't know. If I stay, feeling the way I do, there'll be no avoiding resentment. If you don't stay, wanting to as much as you do—same thing."

"Vicki, dear God! Are you even remotely suggesting separation?"

"I don't *know* what I'm suggesting!" She felt like stamping her feet and pounding the table in frustration. "I can't stand the idea of being away from you for another week, let alone . . . longer. I also can't stand the idea of holding you back, watching you give away a chance like this just because of me, then trying not to hate me for it. But I cannot, after—what? ten days in a country?—adopt it as my own and wave farewell forever to America. To my home!"

The waiter was hovering off to the side, obviously aware

that this was not a conversation to interrupt.

"Joe, so far I've done all the talking and made all the emotional disclosures. I now turn the floor over to you."

Joe felt stunned. Stunned and confused and anguished and, yes, angry. How could she do this to him? Jeopardize this gilt-edged offer, turn it into a two-edged sword that threatened to slice through what he had considered to be impenetrable bonds between them?

"Let's decide what to order," he said. He motioned to the waiter, and they both took a long time over choices. In the market for time again.

Vicki, Vicki, he wanted to bellow, *stop this nonsense and follow me, the way you're supposed to.* He gazed out at the sharp-etched outline of the fortress against the darkening sky. What *he* wanted, at this moment, was yesterday's right, the right that men of ages past had, to demand her fealty. Sure, Lord Beck, his inner voice sneered, fat chance.

"Vicki, I can't believe that you and I are talking about . . . Dear God, what *are* we talking about? Separation? You and I? That's impossible, honey."

"Then what is possible?"

"I don't know. I'm so damned confused. Vicki, I can't let you go. You're the core of my life. But how do I just wave good-bye to this chance Anton has given me? It would be like throwing away the golden egg and killing the goose."

"I'm afraid there is no good decision. Only bad . . . and worse."

He shook his head. His brilliant, top-quality mind was a hopeless jumble. "I'll have to think about this later. I just can't sort it out right now. We'd better order."

He placed the order for a dinner neither of them wanted.

— 10 —

A VOID WAS developing between Joe and Vicki. For both of them, so used to sharing the smallest, least significant of thoughts as well as the larger-than-life issues, the void seemed mammoth, uncrossable.

Vicki had made a decision. She was sure it was the only one she could make. And yet, in many ways, it was worse than no decision at all. It had given shape to the void, which was growing like the San Andreas Fault that shook California with periodic earthquakes. They were headed for an earthquake of their own.

Joe kept trying to address the subject. He formed arguments and made mental lists of reasons why Vicki should reconsider, but when he tried to put his thoughts into words, they came out harshly, as criticism. He was angry with Vicki for not becoming, with great enthusiasm, a one-woman cheering section for his princely job offer, regardless of the side issues. He knew he was being unreasonable. He knew the side issues were far from incidental. He knew he was succumbing to his old ailment, tunnel vision, but the only thing he was sure of was that he didn't know what to do.

The weekend turned out to be packed with activity as well as fraught with tension. On Saturday, Gretchen, clearly under instructions from Anton, offered to take them on another tour. Joe and Vicki grabbed at the chance. For the first time in their lives together, it was easier, and better, to be busy and with other people than to be alone.

They went to the Augustinian Abbey, an exquisite seventeenth-century monastery in the nearby village of St. Florian. Gretchen led them through one magnificent room after another.

"The abbey is built above the tomb of Saint Florian," she explained. "He was killed because he refused to sacrifice to the Roman gods."

"Is there a penalty like that for refusing to sacrifice to the gods of Austria?" Vicki asked the question in a joking tone, but it still earned a scathing look from her husband.

"The fresco on this ceiling depicts the Austrian victory over the Turks." Vicki studied the triumphant Austrians, straight and proud in their saddles, the arrogance of victory on their faces, their vanquished foes fallen behind them. There could be no clear victory in the war that threatened to break out between her and Joe.

They walked across the floor under which Bruckner was buried. He had once been the organist there. So many graves, Vicki thought. I wonder where mine will be. Or have I just dug it?

They barely had time, upon their return to the apartment, to shower and change and rejoin Gretchen, with Conrad this time. They were all to go to the Hollwegs' house for cocktails, then on to yet another restaurant for dinner.

Vicki was exhausted, and the deep lines around Joe's eyes were painfully apparent, but at least when they were surrounded by people the silence didn't thunder in their ears. How awful. How absolutely damned awful to be unable to talk easily to each other, to reach out and touch, to laugh together. How had that all disappeared so quickly? Had she killed their closeness, all by herself? She could imagine how many women would leap at the chance she was resisting. She couldn't help it. She could only deal with the way she was—not with the way she wished she could be.

When Vicki finally, gratefully lay in the huge bed, most of its considerable width separating her from her husband, she thought with dread about the obstacle course they must run tomorrow: the return of Anton.

How would he be told? What would he be told? She hadn't been included in Joe's ruminations. The whole situation was intolerable, an unreal nightmare involving two people whose dreams were usually sunny and joyful.

Much of Sunday was a haze. She and Joe had breakfast on the terrace. The warm sun did nothing to thaw the iciness between them.

"Joe?"

"Yes?"

"What are you going to tell Anton?"

He stared at her, a hurt, angry, confused look on his face. "I'll have to tell him that you're going back to Boston. That I will stay for the time being and start to learn the business, but that we can't give him a definite answer yet."

"What time are you due at the airport to pick him up?"

"Noon."

"Would you like me to go with you?"

"No need to bother. It's not a long trip, and Anton and I have things to discuss. We'll probably have to speak German, so it wouldn't be much fun for you."

She felt a door being solidly shut in her face.

During the two hours that Joe was gone, Vicki wandered around the house, wistfully saying a reluctant good-bye to the child and her kitten, to the Chagall and the Degas and Hercules and the Venezuelan rug—to all the various treasures of a lifestyle she couldn't help but yearn for, but for which she couldn't make sacrificial offerings.

And Anton. How did she say good-bye to him? That complex man who tried to give his love through presents because he didn't seem to know how else to give it. Anton, kind, thoughtful . . . so confident in his business mode, yet rather shy and uncertain with those he cared for deeply. How she hated to hurt Anton. She hoped it was possible, in their limited shared vocabulary, for her to assure him that he was a plus in the option-weighing, not a minus.

Anton was his usual pleasant, considerate self when they arrived. There was no hint in his expression that he'd had a disagreeable discussion with his nephew. In short order the house was once again filled with people: Gretchen, Conrad, Anton, and Anton and Rudolph's sister, who lived with her husband in Vienna, along with their two sons, one daughter-in-law, and grandchildren—a four-year-old boy and a tiny three-month-old girl.

The house hummed with activity. Louisa was in her element, singlehandedly producing one gastronomic delight after another from the kitchen. One after another, Joe's newly met relatives gushed, in sentences formed in articulate to stumbling English, their pleasure in meeting Joe and Vicki, the joy with which they looked forward to having them become a solid part of their family.

Vicki felt like screaming. She felt hemmed in, pressured, guilt-laden. This wasn't right, and it wasn't fair. Why hadn't Joe told Anton that she didn't intend to become a lifetime resident of Austria? Or *had* he told him, and this was a last-ditch attempt to manipulate her into changing her mind?

At last, as the evening ground toward a close and everyone but Gretchen and Conrad had gone home, Anton insisted that they all convene in the living room for a schnapps. Vicki's eyes moved from one to the other: Anton, always the perfect host, doing his best to make everyone happy; Gretchen, to whom he refused to give the one thing that would bring her happiness; Conrad, attractive, quiet, kind, but always a bit distracted, probably thinking of tomorrow's surgery. And Joe. Joe. Her beloved one-mind, one-body, one-need other half, almost visibly severing himself from her.

God, God, what do I do? Do I swallow all my misgivings and follow my husband wherever he leads, as women used to do, just trusting that if he's happy, I'll be happy? But we've never functioned that way, Joe and I. The zeal with which we've supported, even rejoiced in each other's separateness is one of the main things that's brought us closer and closer together. It wouldn't work for me to be a mere shadow of my husband, living in a land that would always feel foreign!

"Vicki?"

She dragged her drifting mind back to concentrate on what Anton was saying. "It distresses me to know that you must once again leave us tomorrow." So Joe *had* told him! Then why—

But Anton's voice continued, "He says the preparations for the moving are taking much time."

Her astonished eyes whipped to Joe's. He gave her a sheepish half-shrug, then dropped his gaze. How could he? How could he push her into a corner like this? Why, he was trying to force her to back down, or to postpone facing the issue. She was too tired for this, too tautly strung to think clearly. Her eyes switched to Gretchen's ashen face, caught in an expression of candid, undisguised anguish. Vicki flipped.

"Uncle Anton." Her tone was sharp-edged, hushed with intensity, her hands tightly clasped as she leaned forward. "I'm afraid Joe hasn't been entirely candid with you." She ignored Joe's intake of breath, avoided his eyes. "The situation is very complicated." Almost immediately, Gretchen began a quick-following translation. "The offer that you have made to Joe, and to me, is generous beyond all belief. You've offered more than we could ever have dreamed of having. Even more than that, you've offered your warmth and your love. I cannot tell you how much all of that means to me. Joe must make his own decision about what he will do, but I have told him, and now I tell you: I cannot live in Austria, not as a full-time, lifelong resident. My own country is too precious to me for that." She forced her eyes to remain locked with Anton's unwavering blue gaze.

"Austria is beautiful and exciting, but it is not my home. My home is America." Her faltering gaze flickered and fell for a moment. "That is the major, but not the only, block for me."

"Vicki!"

She overrode Joe's interjection. "You have a capable, eager daughter who desperately wants what you have so freely offered to my husband."

Gretchen's interpretation stopped. Vicki saw the combination of shock, gratitude, and yes, fear, on her face. Anton's face was a mask of control. His piercing gaze was concentrated totally on her as he urged Gretchen to pick up the translation. After one quick glance at Joe's furious expression, Vicki avoided looking his way and spoke directly to Anton.

"Gretchen, according to what Joe has told me, is considered by all who work for and around her to be an extraordinary businesswoman, and she's paid her dues, as we say in America. She *belongs* here, in every sense of the word. It just doesn't seem fair to me that you're shutting her out and handing all the authority to Joe."

She realized there was a steady stream of tears running down her face. A white handkerchief was thrust into her hand. She nodded with gratitude to Conrad, who smiled at her sympathetically.

"You offer so much, Uncle Anton. And I honestly believe that you have the best of intentions. But you do manipulate people. You do it by dangling very enticing carrots in front of our eyes, and it's amazing how addicted a person can get to carrots. I want them myself, but not enough to give up my homeland and not enough to walk over Gretchen to get them. I'm sorry if I've hurt you, but I had to tell you how I feel.

"Now"—she stumbled to her feet—"I'm going to bed." Before anyone could stop her, she rushed up the steps and into the bedroom, where she ripped off her clothes and threw them onto a chair. Just as she was pulling a nightgown over her head, Joe came stomping into the room. She finished adjusting the gown and faced her furious husband.

"What the hell did you think you were doing?" His face

was red with rage. "Who gave you the right to tell Anton how he should run his business? I hope you're satisfied! Gretchen went home sobbing, Conrad was very upset, and Anton looks as if someone just drained all his blood. And me...well, I'm sure you've just ended my chances, so I suppose that gives you one thing to be happy about."

He stormed past her and took his toothbrush and razor out of the bathroom and grabbed a couple of pillows and an extra blanket from the closet. "I'll sleep on the couch."

Vicki stumbled weakly into bed, burying her head in the pillows so Joe couldn't hear her crying.

Luckily her plane left fairly early the next morning. She deliberately got up late and took as much time as possible packing and dressing. Louisa, her happy smile in place, brought her a breakfast tray. "Your husband is gone to the walk," she cheerily informed Vicki, "and Herr Beck, he says thirty minutes you leave for the airport."

"Thank you, Louisa."

There was practically no conversation on the way to the airport. Joe sat in front with Anton, who insisted on driving. They parked the car and walked to the terminal. Vicki had only one small carry-on bag. To her enormous surprise, when she turned to bid farewell to Anton, he put his arms around her and held her for a moment, silently, then gently placed a kiss on her cheek.

"Thank you, Victoria."

She stared at him in amazement. "You're thanking me? What for?"

"The honesty. So brave a thing, and so rare. Fly safely with God."

He looked at her for a moment, then turned quickly away and walked back out to his car. She could have sworn she saw moisture in his eyes. She and Joe just looked at each other, through all the layers of confusion that had grown like thick, virulent weeds in so short a time.

"Good-bye, Joe." Vicki could scarcely speak. What did her good-bye mean? How long would this separation last? She couldn't bear to think about it.

"Good-bye, Vicki."

There were no messages of any kind to read in his eyes. It was the first time she could ever remember their looking flat and devoid of life. They stared at each other for a long, long moment, then turned, almost simultaneously, to go in opposite directions.

Vicki prayed for an extra surge of jet power this time. Her heart felt so heavy she feared it would weigh the plane down. *Joe, Joe Joe!* A million molecules, tissues, cells seemed to join together in a resounding inner chorus of demand. *I need you, need you, need you!* The plane soared up, off, farther and farther away.

Monday night, Tuesday, Tuesday night, Wednesday— the days dragged by like misty cloud banks, foggy, obscure. She moved through the squares of time with robotlike fixation, a pawn on a no-win game board. She talked to her parents briefly and talked to Joe's parents briefly—stilted conversations that effectively disguised any real emotional disclosures. They gave their love, their concern; that was all they could give. They couldn't give her Joe, or her life the way it had been before the letter from Anton.

Their life the way it had been: full of financial pressures, time squeezes, impossible deadlines. But full also of free give-and-take, of pulling together, of equal say and equal effort, of love . . . oh, so full of love. Until the letter from Anton. And what did the letter bring? An offer of a better job than Joe had envisioned, the promise of wealth and flexibility to travel and ready-made friends and relatives eager to enfold them into their close-knit group.

All that glitters . . . Now why had that come to mind? Why indeed. It *was* gold, wasn't it? The sought-after golden opportunity. The only flaw in the shiny surface was her. Why couldn't she just take a chance? Because they weren't dealing with chance; they were dealing with certainty. You simply couldn't turn a midwestern, all-American, down-home girl into an internationalist permanently stationed in Austria. So where did that leave the aforementioned girl? Nowhere. And was nowhere a better place to live than

Austria? How in heaven did she answer that? She had needed time to think, but her thoughts were a huge, mangled, unreadable mess.

She went to the bathroom for some aspirin to counter the ache that seemed to have taken up permanent residence in her head. The medicine cabinet door made its usual loud squeak as it opened and repeated its lament on closing. Vicki hesitated, wondering if there had been another noise in the apartment. "No," she mumbled, putting the two tablets into her mouth and washing them down with the city water with its slight taste of chlorine. "Look at me, jumping at imaginary noises. After years of city living I should be used to noise."

She stepped into the bedroom and yelped. Joe stood before her, his battered suitcase on the floor to his right, and the duffel bag to the left. He looked tired and crumpled and creased.

"Oh, Joe, did I ruin it for you? Did Anton send you away?"

He shook his head slowly, his eyes never leaving her. Vicki was frightened, the enormity of what she might have done to him descending on her.

In two long strides he crossed to her and pulled her into his arms. "Vicki, Vicki. I've missed you so. Just let me hold you for a minute, until I can really believe we're together."

He kissed her, deeply, hungrily. She clung to him, her arms strong with desperation. Why was he here? How long could she keep him close to her? She shivered, half with the pleasure of being held in his familiar arms, his lips on hers, and half with the dread that it might only be temporary.

Joe felt the shudder run through her body. He pressed her to him more tightly, willing the fear and the hurt away, willing the fissures to heal. How was he to tell her of the twists and turns of the path his mind had traveled before reaching his moment of truth? He knew her so well; she was bound to take the blame, even though it didn't belong to her. He raised his head and gazed at her, letting his eyes verify the message that his body was sending to his brain: Vicki was here in his arms. Everything would be all right.

"Oh, honey, I've been half crazy since you left." She felt him shudder as he held her. "I just couldn't think at first. So much happened to us so fast. Vicki, please. Just look at me and say that you love me. I need so badly to hear you say those words."

"I love you, I love you, I love you." She didn't care that she was getting the front of his shirt wet.

"Honey, I have so much to tell you." He looked into her deep green eyes, missing the dancing lights, wanting desperately to restore the happy sparkle. "It's all right, darling, it really is. Anton did *not* send me away. I came back because I had to. No place can be home without you. And Vicki"—he concentrated his gaze on hers, his mind entreating her to listen, to believe—"you were right, you know."

The green eyes widened. "What do you mean?"

"Let's sit down." He took her hand and led her into the living room, where they settled side by side on the sofa. Joe pulled her tightly against him, his arm around her, his hand clutching her shoulder. It helped stabilize him, helped give him the feeling that they couldn't be separated again. "Vicki, do you realize how much has happened to us in less than two months? And I think we'd agree that at first it seemed like a dream come true."

Her eyes dropped. "Yes, but dreams have a way of ending when you wake up."

"Vicki, look at me. It's important that you understand what I'm saying, and even more important that you believe it. You and I were both caught up in what seemed like a miracle. But reality hit you sooner than it hit me. I wanted the dream so, honey. I really did. So much so that I shut things out of my mind, the very things you put into words the last night you were at Anton's."

"Joe—"

"No, let me finish. When you left the first time, I almost went nuts, I was so damned lonesome. But I knew you were coming back, and I kept telling myself that I'd talk you into staying. I also kept telling myself that your absence was the only thing bothering me." Joe stood and paced back and forth in front of her. "You know how many times you've told me how envious you are of my so-called mental discipline?"

"Yes."

He stopped and faced her. "It's not all good, hon. Sometimes it just allows you to be dishonest with yourself for a longer period."

Vicki sat, trying to be patient, needing to know what he was leading up to.

He dropped back onto the sofa beside her. "It would take hours to tell you all the processes my brain had to go through to clear the view. I guess it was too dazzled by that large pot of gold. The problem, as you said, was location."

Her heart stopped.

"The end of the rainbow *was* in the wrong country. I already knew how incomplete I felt without you. The rest of it is what I hadn't acknowledged. It wasn't just you I missed. I missed being at *home* with you. And home is, as you have said all along, here in America."

Vicki stared at him, trying to speak. He was coming back to her, on her terms, and attempting to make it sound like his free decision. She was getting what she wanted, and she felt sick about it.

"And the other part, Vicki, the part about Gretchen. How could I have closed my mind to what was happening to her? It's terrible what greed can do to you."

"Oh, Joe, my darling, I was so afraid I'd lost you!" She slid tightly against him, safe in the haven of his arms. "I want so very desperately for you to have everything that's important to you. After all those years of working together so you'd have the right education for a good job, I never dreamed it was possible that *I* might force you to forfeit what has to be the best offer you'll ever get!"

"Vicki." His hands went to her shoulders and forced her away just far enough for him to look into her eyes. "You didn't force me to forfeit anything. You only forced me to face the truth. You must believe me."

But she didn't.

"And now"—Joe stood up and hunched his shoulders in an attempt to ease the tight, travel-locked muscles—"I feel as if I have a double layer of dust on me. I need a good shower." His grin was a little strained. "Or at least as good a shower as I can get in our tin cube."

At her immediate wince, he stood squarely before her, his stern gaze capturing hers, "I'm only kidding, Vicki. You mustn't jump on my every remark. I'm exactly where I want to be." Leaning over to kiss her on the lips, he added, "Honestly."

She still couldn't believe him.

She fixed a simple meal, which they ate in relative silence at the tiny, scarred kitchen table. The silence was understandable—Joe was too tired to talk—but it was still hard on Vicki. She wondered if this heavy weight would leave her. Despite all his assurances, she felt like a murderess who had slain his dream.

As soon as Joe finished eating, he collapsed into bed. Vicki hurriedly cleaned up the dishes, then went to the bedroom and quickly removed her clothes, eager to slide into his arms to renew their too long suspended passion. She exhaled her pleasure as he pulled her close to his warm body, sighing, "Vicki, Vicki . . ."

She raised her lips for his kiss, but, to her dismay, he was fast asleep. She lay there for a long time, letting her skin get used to the feel of his once again, so many fears running through her mind. Would he be able, one day, to truly forgive her? Was this just weariness, or would their passion for each other be dimmed by the loss of his dream.

She knew that she wouldn't be able to sleep for hours, but there was no way she could leave the bed, leave the circle of his arms. She had no idea what the future would bring, but right now she'd settle for simply being with him.

The moment he awoke the following morning, all doubts about passion were dispelled. They made love hungrily, frantically, desperate to kiss, hold, touch, caress each other. Vicki was late for her first appointment.

Joe started the job-hunting circuit immediately, despite Vicki's admonitions to rest for a few days. He seemed driven to find something, to "get settled." When she came home late Thursday afternoon, he had letters and files and papers stacked around him on the kitchen table.

She leaned over to kiss his cheek. "I still can't see why you don't at least wait until Monday. Taking one weekend off isn't sinful, you know."

He smiled up at her. "I know. But I'm eager to get started. We've lived in this crummy apartment long enough. It'll be nice to be able to move into something decent and really get our lives rolling."

If he noticed the pained expression on Vicki's face at the mention of the "crummy" apartment, he didn't acknowledge it. She set her bag of groceries on the sink and started unpacking it. "I picked up a chicken and some zucchini for dinner. I hope you're hungry."

"I'm starved. But hon?"

She turned. "What?"

"Can you save that for tomorrow night? Let's go out for dinner. It would be fun to go to Jimmy's or Pier Four or one of the old standbys."

Whose old standbys? she wondered. Eating at those restaurants had never been possible on their budget. "But—" She stopped, the automatic warning that they couldn't afford it sticking in her throat. They'd work it out. She'd been enough of a killjoy already.

"Oh, by the way, Anton sends his love."

She whirled. "Anton? When did you talk to him?"

"I called him this morning. I left Austria in kind of a hurry and didn't have a chance to fully explain my reasons or to thank him for all he did for us. Or tried to do. Anyway, that's taken care of. Finis."

Her heart a hard lump in her chest, she studied his expression, searching for a clue to his real feelings. Damn. No wonder he wanted to go out to a fancy restaurant—just talking to Anton was enough to create an illusion of solvency. But Joe was once again hard at work, reviewing contacts, making lists of prospects—first, second, third, and on down the list. There was no need to remind herself that, given free choice, the name that would doubtless fill all those spaces would be Beck Metals Corporation. Swallowing hard, she put the food into the refrigerator.

Joe had remarkable success in setting up appointments. At least it was reassuring to be reminded how employable he was. By the end of the first full week he had two solid job offers, excellent offers with top-flight companies.

He was beginning to regret that he'd ever gone to Austria, ever been exposed to Beck Metals Corporation. The brief glimpse he'd caught of the exciting future he'd have had there couldn't help but color his enthusiasm for these alternatives. Making a decision to accept one of the positions at hand would require more than a little of his famous mental discipline. Oh, well, he had several other interviews scheduled for the coming week, so at least he could shelve the matter for a while longer.

The other problem that worried him was Vicki's obvious inability to accept the reasons he had given for his return. He found himself weighing words, taking care with joking remarks. Any reference to their low-budget living standard or to his frustration about his interviews brought an automatic response from his wife: a wince, or quickly blinked back tears, or a nervous change of subject.

The truth was that he felt exactly as he'd told her he felt. Whether he'd have the strength of character to face the facts without Vicki to prod him was an unknown. But he was sure of one thing: If he hadn't faced them when he did, he'd have been forced to do so later. He was ashamed of the way he had closed his mind to the unfairness of Gretchen's plight, and as for the rest . . . he really didn't want to leave this country permanently either.

Joe pushed aside the notepad on which he had been recording his impressions of the morning's appointment. He was sitting at the table in the kitchen; it was the cheeriest place in the apartment in the daytime. Of course nothing in this dump was cheerful when Vicki was gone.

His mind automatically clicked to "caution." Before Austria, he and Vicki used to joke all the time about "the dump." If he made any such remark around her now, he'd see that hurt look on her face. Damn. Maybe they should go out again that night. No, not a good idea. He'd just get Vicki worried about the budget again. He should worry, too; they weren't exactly loaded. One more fact to face. It was time for him to get back to earth. He returned to his notes.

When Vicki got home from work she found Joe asleep on the couch. It was a rare sight. Joe almost never took naps. She tiptoed into the bedroom and changed into jeans, then quietly crossed to the kitchen. Just as she reached for the refrigerator door she heard, "Hey! Don't touch anything in there!"

Before she could reply, Joe had appeared in the doorway, sleepily rubbing his eyes. "Hi, honey." He gave her a smile that was interrupted by a yawn, then pulled her into his arms. "Mmm, how nice to wake up and find a sexy woman in my kitchen."

"How nice to come home and find a handsome man on my couch. You woke up just in time. I was about to attack."

"Don't let me stop you. I'll return to my former position. I'm always up for a little sex before dinner."

"It may be *instead* of dinner, particularly if you're not going to allow me to touch anything in here."

"Now that I'm in here, all rules are changed. But as far as dinner is concerned, there's food, and then there's food."

"I suspect that's a thinly veiled naughty remark."

"I'm willing to take off the veil. In fact, I'm willing to uncover everything."

He kissed her deeply, his hands grasping her and pulling her close. "Have we ever made love on the kitchen floor?"

"Oh, no, here we go again. What's the matter with a nice, comfortable bed?"

"Damn Sam, what a drag. A wife with no sense of adventure."

Vicki jerked back, ever so slightly, but enough too show that the remark had hurt.

Joe dropped his hands, a slow anger building. He went to the refrigerator and got the bottle of good white wine he'd gone out for earlier. He took the corkscrew out of the drawer and removed the cork. "Could you get the glasses, Vicki? I put them in the freezer to chill."

She took out the glasses and set them on the counter, watching him warily. What had caused the sudden change of mood?

As Joe filled each of them he spoke in a strangely controlled tone. "I picked up some stuffed fillet of sole from the fish market down the street, and I made a salad, so dinner's all ready."

"Joe! How nice!" She took the offered glass. "Any special occasion?"

He stood and looked at her for a moment. "Well, there wasn't anything special, but maybe there should be."

Vicki felt very apprehensive. "What do you mean?"

"Come on, let's sit down." He led her to the sofa, where they sat side by side on the crushed cushions. "First, let's drink to us and to our future together."

Vicki's gaze dropped for a split second; then she clinked her glass with Joe's and took a sip.

Joe's vibrant blue eyes held hers as he took a long swallow of the cold wine. Then he set his glass on the coffee table and spoke in a steady, firm voice. "Vicki, I'm getting damned tired of your attitude."

"What?" Her eyes widened in surprise. "My attitude about what?"

"You've decided to take all the blame for my not taking the job in Austria, and frankly it's become a pain in the neck. Number one, I did not lie to you. I told you exactly why I did what I did. But by doing the long-suffering number—"

"Joe, I haven't—"

"Yes, you have. You just did. I couldn't even toast our future without getting a pained expression. Vicki, don't you see what you're doing? You're robbing me of the right to express my feelings freely. Sure I wanted the job with Anton. Who wouldn't? But I want it here, in my own country, and I want it without clobbering Gretchen. And I can't have it that way. It's hard to get excited about some of the other positions I've looked at, but that will pass. Vicki, you wanted a lot of it, too; you can't deny that. So why can't we share that disappointment, as we've shared everything else?"

She took another sip of the wine, trying to completely understand what he was saying. "What have I been doing?"

"You get visibly upset about the damnedest things: a remark about this apartment, for instance, even though *you're* the one who used to call it a dump all the time. I can't even discuss my job possibilities with you, because you immediately start to apologize for wrecking my big chance."

He took her glass and set it beside his, then held both of her hands. "One of the wonderful things I've been sure of ever since we got married is that whatever happened, we were in it together. Vicki, my darling, darling Vicki, the future belongs to the two of us. You and me, remember? For better and for worse. If we're going to sing the blues, hon, let's make it a duet."

She sat, quietly stunned. "I didn't realize, I really didn't. Oh, Joe, I'm so sorry—"

"Ahh!" He held up his hand. "For Pete's sake, no more apologies!"

She grinned, the sparkle returning to her eyes. "Okay, no more apologies." She threw her arms around his neck, looking up at him adoringly. "Oh, Joe, we're really home, aren't we? We're home and we're together. The future is bound to take care of itself!"

"No question about it. We'll wake up tomorrow morning and pretend we're back where we were the day after my graduation, with the world out there beckoning. And we'll discuss all the job possibilities and weigh the pros and cons and make a mutual decision. Agreed?"

"Agreed." .

"Now. Why don't we put this wine back in the fridge and go to bed?"

"No question about it; we're back to normal. Your mind has returned to sex."

They had put away the wine and were headed for the

bedroom when the doorbell rang. Joe frowned. "Who could that be? Let's not answer."

The bell sounded again.

"Joe, I think we'd better. What if there's a problem?"

"Oh, okay." With great reluctance, he crossed to the door and opened it.

There in the hallway stood Anton and Gretchen.

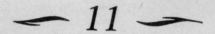

11

"Uncle Anton!"

"Josef. How are you? We are coming to talk to you."

"Oh...yes, of course. Come in, come in. Gretchen, how are you?" Joe was stumbling over his words. Vicki was impressed by the fact that he could talk at all. She was just plain struck dumb.

Gretchen came directly to her and gave her a warm hug and a kiss on the cheek. "Vicki, it is so good to see you."

"Thank you...I mean, it's nice to see you, too, I mean, this is a real surprise!"

Joe had recovered enough from his initial shock to experience another. "Anton! You *flew* here?" Anton's distrust of air travel was legendary.

Anton nodded. "Yes. With my Gretchen being at my side, it is not so much a fearful thing."

For the first time, Vicki noticed the new glow on Gretchen's face, the interchange of laughing, loving glances between father and daughter. "Oh, forgive us. We're both so flustered we haven't even asked you to sit down."

Anton looked delighted. "We are surprising you, yes?"

"That's an understatement." Vicki started to fluff up the couch cushions, then shrugged. They were beyond hope. "Can I get you a glass of wine?"

After another quick exchange of glances, Gretchen said, "We'd love some."

Vicki blessed Joe's impulsiveness in buying a bottle of good wine that day. She also blessed their failure to drink it. By the time she returned with four glasses, everyone had settled down. "Here. I'm afraid the wineglasses all have chips in them, so be careful." Vicki was amazed at how glad she was to see them again, and the pleasure of Gretchen's warm greeting clung to her still.

"Thank you, Victoria. Now." Anton held the glass high. "I toast. To all of us. And to the new program!"

Completely befuddled, Joe and Vicki joined the toast.

Anton held his glass by the stem, the base balanced on his knee. "There is much to be telling. I wish to say it by my own words. I must be learning better the English"—here he actually winked at Vicki—"and I am thinking that Victoria must be learning the German."

Vicki sat very, very still, aware that this was a matter of consequence.

Anton continued, his expression serious now. "You know, to love your country, that is a"—there was a momentary hesitation—"a natural thing. It comes from the heart." His eyes clouded. "There was a time . . . when it was difficult for me . . ." He cleared his throat. "But my country was my country. It is a human need, you know, to belong somewhere."

Vicki blinked. She realized how much of himself Anton was sharing. She also realized, to her surprise, that Anton's English was more certain than before. Could it be that he was more at ease with them?

"And"—his Joe-blue eyes looked straight into Vicki's—"you said, at my house, the truth about my Gretchen." She watched him swallow laboriously. "It is my shame that I was not even knowing what were her needs."

Gretchen reached over to place her hand on her father's. Vicki was in imminent danger of weeping.

"So." His back straightened. "We arrive at the new program. And now it is best for Gretchen to be telling you."

"Yes." Gretchen's voice cracked. She stopped for a moment, took a sip of her wine, and continued. "Joe, my father and I would like you to join the firm. You would have to move to Hartford, Connecticut, since that is the present location of the U.S. division. There have been plans for some time to have two management centers for the company. It makes sense that one would be in America."

Joe looked as if he just might faint.

"We would be—what is the word?" Her sparkling gaze flicked to Vicki and back to Joe. "Co-conspirators?"

Joe and Vicki both laughed at the same time, an explosion of happy tension.

Anton again took over. "There is a"—he looked at Gretchen—"codicil?"

She laughed. "I think he means there is a catch."

Vicki wasn't sure she could breathe. She felt as if she'd been caught in a tornado, flipped from one unexpected location to the next, and it wasn't over yet.

"All right, the catch. We must require from you a year, maybe two years, in Austria. It is where you are having to learn the business." Anton, for the first time since she'd known him, looked anxious.

Joe's eyes darted to hers. They weren't hard to read now. They were asking, *Please, please.*

She had no problem with her answer. "Of course. I'd love to live in Austria for a couple of years. It's all in knowing that I *can* come home again."

They all broke out in happy chatter, excited, relieved.

Finally Vicki remembered her manners. "We have plenty of food. Will you stay for dinner?"

"No, thank you." Anton stood. "On that airplane, they are feeding and feeding us. And I am eating it all; it makes me not so nervous." They all laughed, a communion of happiness. He extended a hand to help Vicki out of the sagging chair, then put his arm around her shoulders as they walked toward the door. "And Vicki, I have been thinking. While you are learning the German, you should be planning a new program. There is that problem in our company. So many women, they are working. And they have at home the children. It is causing much troubles. Maybe we should be having the . . ." He squinted.

"Counseling service," Gretchen interjected.

"Yes, that is it."

Vicki grinned up at him. "Uncle Anton, you are a smooth operator."

His smile was warm and knowing. "The carrot, it works two ways. If the rabbit is not wanted, the carrot is not dangled." He gave her shoulder a squeeze. "We see you tomorrow, then we go for seven days to stay with Rudolph and Maria. They take us to Disney World!"

They all laughed at the thought of Anton in Disney World. "My Gretchen, she does more and more the work, so I have more the time for play. Clever, right? The manipulating?" His grin, directed straight at Vicki, was downright devilish.

As soon as the door closed behind them, Joe picked Vicki up and swung her in a wide circle. "Hallelujah!"

"I don't believe it." Vicki stood unsteadily from the whirl. "I just don't believe it."

"We're golden, Vicki, we're golden!"

She shook her head, then grinned in incredulous wonder. "You're right. You're absolutely right!"

He still looked stunned. "Vicki, I feel as if we've not only found the end of the rainbow, but we're holding the pot of gold!"

She kissed his cheek. "Weren't we on the way to our bed when we were so politely interrupted?"

"We sure were. I can't think of a better way to celebrate!"

As they walked out of the room, arm in arm, she sang, "Oh, it must be gold, 'cause brass don't glitter like that . . . Yeah, Yeah . . . It must be gold 'cause brass don't glitter like that . . ." She looked up at him. "Joe?"

"Hmm?"

"Congratulations."

She saw the flash of his happy smile. "Same to you, lady. As usual, we brought it off together."

"Thanks, hon. And Joe?"

"Yes, darling?"

"I'm glad you bawled me out earlier. I'm glad we knew we'd be just fine in any case."

Their eyes held. "So am I. No matter what, even in 'richer,' our love is the important thing. That's the rainbow."

"I love you."

"I love you, too."

All of the above titles are $1.95

Prices may be slightly higher in Canada.

Available at your local bookstore or return this form to:

SECOND CHANCE AT LOVE
Book Mailing Service
P.O. Box 690, Rockville Centre, NY 11571

Please send me the titles checked above. I enclose _____ Include 75¢ for postage
and handling if one book is ordered; 25¢ per book for two or more not to exceed
$1.75. California, Illinois, New York and Tennessee residents please add sales tax.

NAME_____

ADDRESS_____

CITY_____STATE/ZIP_____

(allow six weeks for delivery)   **SK-41b**

HERE'S WHAT READERS ARE SAYING ABOUT

To Have and to Hold™

"Your TO HAVE AND TO HOLD series is a fabulous and long overdue idea."
— *A. D., Upper Darby, PA**

"I have been reading romance novels for over ten years and feel the TO HAVE AND TO HOLD series is the best I have read. It's exciting, sensitive, refreshing, well written. Many thanks for a series of books I can relate to."
— *O. K., Bensalem, PA**

"I enjoy your books tremendously."
— *J. C., Houston, TX**

"I love the books and read them over and over."
— *E. K., Warren, MI**

"You have another winner with the new TO HAVE AND TO HOLD series."
— *R. P., Lincoln Park, MI**

"I love the new series TO HAVE AND TO HOLD."
— *M. L., Cleveland, OH**

"I've never written a fan letter before, but TO HAVE AND TO HOLD is fantastic."
— *E. S., Narberth, PA**